Atonement

Samara Reed

Samara Reed

Samara Reed

This one is dedicated to all the girlies who think they are unlovable, and who can't quite muster up the courage to find out if it's not true.
Your person is out there, and it's never too late. Take it from Ginger. Someone is going to come along and rock your world. In the meantime...say hello to Dane for me.

Atonement play list:

Curiosities by Bryce Savage
The Bad Angel by Nikki Idol
Promises by Emo
Chills (Dark version) by Mickey Valen & Joey Myron
You Put A Spell On Me - Austin Giorgio
Let the World Burn by Chris Grey
Like You Mean It by Steven Rodriguez
Love Me by Ex Habit
Desires by Meg Meyers

CHAPTER ONE

Dane

"I'm coming!" I hear a woman yell from somewhere beyond the darkness. My fingers drum along the counter as I count. Twenty-one, twenty-two, twenty-three. I ring the bell again; I am not a patient man.

"I said I'm comin'!" she yells with a little more gusto as she emerges from the doorway, completely black one moment, but filled with her curly red hair and bright jumpsuit the next.

"What can I do ya for, tall, dark and impatient?" She flips a few pages of the book she places on the counter in front of her and looks up at me, snapping a bubble with her gum.

"I'm looking for Jack."

"Jack ain't here. And even if he was, he don't do men. I don't think I have anyone open today who does."

What in the hell is that supposed to mean? "I had it on pretty good authority that Jack can be found here."

She looks up at me more intently, drinking me in from my chest up to my hair. "What brings ya in babe? Maybe I can help ya out?"

"Doubtful." I grunt. "I need to see Jack." Her head quirks at me and her eyebrows draw in before they shoot up. As she watches me, she paws at the counter until she hits a cell phone. She picks it up and dials, never taking her eyes off me until the call connects.

"Jackie baby, there's someone here askin' for ya." Her gaze lifts back to me and she nods once. "What's yer name?"

I cross my arms and pin her with a stare.

"He's a man of few words, I'm afraid. Yeah." She nods while narrowing her eyes at me. "Already done. Yeah. Tall, dark hair, kinda looks like a blast from the past walked in my door, Jack."

Ah, so she noticed. It doesn't usually take long when people are familiar with a Fitzpatrick. If you've seen one, you'd recognize them all. Her recognition tells me I'm on the right track after all.

Abruptly she shoves the phone in my face. "Here ya' go."

"Hello, Jack." I barely get his name out before he's in my ear with his low, angry growl.

"Don't give me any shit. Who's this? Dane? What the hell are you doing at Ginger's?"

"'Oh, hello, Dane. So nice to hear your voice again. Wish I were there to see you, little cousin. Hope you're well.' Geez, would it kill you to inquire as to my health for two seconds?"

"What do you want?" *No amusement whatsoever, go figure.* I spend all this time tracking down my cousin and he just gives me attitude.

"I want out of the family business. And a little birdie told me if I could find you, you could help me with that."

The line goes silent for several moments before he sighs. "I haven't gotten anyone out in five years. And you're different. I don't even know if I could get you out."

"Not good enough. You pulled out friends, they weren't even blood!" I yell through the line. The woman on the other side of the counter, Ginger I'm assuming, jumps back a step and two very large men appear through the blackened doorway. I look at them and lower my voice. "It's worse, Jack."

"What happened?"

"Your dad happened. Thinks he owns us all. I'll do a lot of things, but I won't force myself on someone who doesn't want to marry me."

Jack curses and it sounds distant, like he pulled the phone away from his ear.

"How do I know I can trust you?" he asks after a beat of silence, his indifferent tone pissing me off.

"Because it's just me here, Jack, and I'm not raining hell down on this pretty redhead. I want out. And when I can get my shit in order, I want to pull all the women out, too. It's time you shared the ivory tower you stole with the needy. And the needy happen to have kids they didn't ask for from men they told no, so I hope you have room."

"Put Ginger back on." The authoritarian in him has come to the surface and I can almost picture his stone-cold business face. He won't admit it, but that's a family face.

"Here you go, babe." I pass the phone to Ginger with a wink, and she blows another bubble at me without a trace of humor in her expression.

"I'll find out. No problem." The glare she shoots me could burn a hole through my skull if she had lasers in her head instead of those gorgeous gold and green eyes.

"Where ya stayin'?" Her tone is dead as she hangs up the phone and fixes her gaze back to me, there's no hint of actual interest in it.

"Did I do something I'm not yet aware of? I'm pretty sure I'm just looking for some long lost family and you're providing rather unsavory customer service, Red."

"Not my job to make sure ya get a pleasant experience, guy. My men handle that. It is my job to make sure my men are safe though. And with yous standin' there, I'm not so sure. So, I'm gonna ask ya again; where ya stayin'?"

"I haven't sorted that out. I figured I would follow my lead first and find somewhere to rest my head second. There's a hotel down the block. That seems like as good a place as any."

She snaps her fingers behind her and a third man appears from the darkness beside the other two, stepping forward. It's a little eerie how still and silent they all are, and it makes me wonder if Jack trained them. "Why dontcha take Mr.–"

"The name's Dane." I answer her pointed expression.

She shrugs one shoulder and continues, "Dane, upstairs and let him pick a room. Jack doesn't want him traceable."

"Traceable?"

"Yer cards, kid."

I raise an eyebrow and pull the rolled-up bundle of fifties out of my pocket. "Cards are for idiots. I'm fine. I don't need charity."

"Seems to me ya' do if yous calling in favors it don't sound like yer owed. And ya shouldn't be walkin' around here with all that cash on ya. That makes you the idiot in this room. Follow James and no arguin'. I don't have time for no sass today. Just do it."

I have more questions, but she doesn't stay to listen to them. She pushes a bag into James' hands and spins around, disappearing back through the dark doorway, the remaining two guys following her. I look at James and he crosses his arms over his broad chest, one eyebrow arched, daring me to not listen.

I relent with a sigh. I may as well ride this out for a bit. If I don't, I have a feeling I won't be seeing my cousin and as much as I hate to lean on another Fitzpatrick at any point and in any way; I need him.

CHAPTER TWO

Dane

"Upstairs" turns out to be up several flights of stairs. Forty-two stairs to be exact. Always know how far you have to go to leave a scene - Fitzpatrick 101. Because no one's coming to get you if you get caught.

James opens a door and holds his hand out to usher me inside. Trouble is, the hall is really damn narrow, so going through the door means I have to squeeze past him and the squeeze is *very* tight. He stares me down the whole time I make my way past, my nose just inches from his own. *What is with everyone in this place and staring?*

I'm not sure what I was expecting to walk into, but a massive common space wasn't it. The high ceilings are flooded with light from the large, storefront style windows. This is an old building, and it looks like it's mostly been maintained as such. The exterior walls around the windows are still brick, and the interior walls are a bright, painted white with simple decor. There's several black leather pieces of furniture strewn around the room, all facing a large flat screen mounted between two windows.

A kitchen appears to be behind a breakfast bar to the right and there's a hall leading off to the left. A blonde man looks up from the laptop he's typing on in one of the leather chairs.

"What's up, bro?" He nods toward me and then his eyes shift behind me before I sense James come up to my back soundlessly. "James. Haven't seen you in a while."

A grunt sounds and James brushes past me, his fist held out where the other man is able to bump it.

"Who'd you bring with you?"

"Ginger offered him a spot here. Sounds to me like Jack's gonna be around later."

A look passes over the blonde man's face that I can't decipher. As I'm studying him trying to decide what it is, a flicker of recognition hits me. The hair is different, but the face is familiar, though I can't determine how. I rack my brain, willing it to spark up something else and falling completely short.

"What did you say your name was?" I ask him, interrupting whatever he had started to say to James.

"I didn't," he says simply, grabbing the bag from James' hand and nodding down the hall.

James takes his position behind me again and nudges me forward with a hand on my shoulder. I'm beginning to wonder if this is a prison or an apartment and where the hell I walked into downstairs. This certainly wasn't what I expected and is absolutely the same behavior that's starting at the Fitzpatrick compound. I don't really care to go back to all that, but I follow anyway, letting my luck play out.

The room we're led to is at the end of one very long hallway. I'm surprised by how large the apartment is considering how small the space looked downstairs. This business and apartment must run several buildings back. I count my steps out of habit, timing the walk through the hall for backtracking.

The man we're following turns through a doorway and James steers me the same way from behind. The room is fairly large, with a bed on each side. Dressers mirror one another at the foot of each bed and a couch lines one wall with another door beside it that I can only guess is a closet or a bathroom. One of the beds is made up of dark blue blankets and the other is dressed only in a white fitted sheet. It reminds me of a dorm room, something I never had the distinct pleasure of experiencing and I'm okay with that.

"The only bed that's left is in my room. If you didn't bring anything with you there's always a spare pillow and blanket floating around here somewhere. Laundry's at the end of the hall, bathroom is directly across. I prefer lights out at nine because I get up before the sun." He pauses and looks at me from head to toe again. "Though I'm not sure I'm interested in arguing with you about it."

He waves his hand and flops on his bed, arms stretched out under his head. I turn to look at James and he raises an eyebrow at me.

"Alright. Where do I find this floating pillow then?"

"Just kidding, man." He chuckles and comes back to his feet, already halfway to the other door.

Yanking it open, it does, in fact, look like a closet. He stands on the edge of the lip and reaches into the overhead shelf where it disappears behind the wall, only to come out with a vacuum sealed bag of pillows. "You do have to scrounge up a blanket though, wasn't kidding on that."

He tosses the pack of pillows on the bed in front of me and unzips it before dumping the contents out where they slowly expand. "Dealer's choice." He thrusts his hand forward. "Damien Grohl."

I look down at the hand he put between us before firmly shaking it. I tighten my grip when he slackens his hold. "Grohl? Like Ansel Grohl?"

His eyes squint and his head cocks before he looks at our hands still together, but no longer moving. He grunts and yanks his hand out of mine.

"We might share a name but I'm nothing 'like' him. That old man shook a few screws loose a long time ago." He's not wrong. My dad's favorite general is Ansel Grohl, and he's not only dangerous, he's also unpredictable.

"Agreed." I nod. "That's why I'm here."

It's his turn to study me. He looks a little slower this time before he pushes the hair off my face and his eyes get wide. "Holy shit. Kid Fitzpatrick. I thought you looked like someone, but my brain wouldn't catch up. What the hell are you doing here?"

"Long story I'm not interested in sharing. And the name's Dane." Swatting his hand away, I shove past him and start squeezing pillows. They're soft and I'm kind of pissed about it. Being forced up here felt like a punishment and now I'm wondering what else it is given the state of the *not* prison pillows I'm holding in my hands.

I raise my chin to the ceiling and exhale. My temper isn't going to help me any. I'd scream into one of these luxurious pillows but I'm in a room with two other men and it feels like it's shrinking. *Damnit.*

"Cool. Well, I'll leave you to it, Dane. Me and James here have a few things to talk about in the living room. Just come back down the hall when you're ready, man." Damien is busy trying to turn James around as he speaks to me over his shoulder and I work to suppress a smile at the sight of him backing up James, who is easily six inches taller and wider than him.

With one last look at me James ducks through the door and Damien follows him. I fluff the pillow a little rougher than what's necessary and throw it at the top of the bed before grabbing the bag Red left with James. Inside I find towels and hygiene things. Plain deodorant, travel hair care, a comb, a very boring toothbrush that's nothing like what I prefer. Simple, but I'm impressed none-the-less. Maybe I did find what I'm looking for after all. The question then becomes who I really need help from; Jack, or the feisty redhead downstairs.

I drop the bag next to the dresser as I make my way out of the room, taking a moment to peek into each doorway I pass on my way back to the main space. If anyone else is here right now, they're hidden away well.

"Question," I ask as I cross the threshold into the room. Both men look up at me simultaneously and I get that same eerie feeling I did downstairs at their perfectly synced response time. "What the fuck did I walk into?"

"Assuming you were downstairs first, Ginger's. Hell, this is still Ginger's." Damien beams a little, amused by his own bad joke.

"This isn't a normal landlord situation, and I know where you came from, smartass. How did you get out?"

Damien's face drops. "You know how I got out."

"You're right, I do. I was there wondering why the hell it was only the few of you and not the rest of us, too. How did you *stay* out? Why did they never look for you?"

"What are you trying to do here, kid?" Damien's face shutters, all emotion gone, forming a completely blank slate save for the tick in his jaw.

"I'm trying to bring it all down. You all left too many people behind, and not enough negotiators. There's no one to say no and the people who try to are met with force. You got out and it's all sunshine and rainbows, but you forgot about the people left that didn't have a choice on whether they were there or not. We grew up and got stuck."

His arms drop from where they were crossed over his chest which deflates. "What happened?"

"The higher ups decided they were tired of waiting for the young people to fall in love and started picking who was getting married and when. No one gets a choice in the matter and the women's cycles are being monitored. They're tired of waiting for more children so they're making them on their own schedule."

"And who's directly responsible for that decision?" Damien and I both turn to the voice coming from the door. There stands Jack, unmistakable given the strong lineage that makes all Fitzpatricks look like various versions of each other. Jack looks like a younger version of his dad, Russell, a fact that I've heard eats at him and probably what drives him to the longer hair that's cropped just above his ears rather than the standard military cut his dad personally cuts all the men's hair in.

"Who do you think?" I don't mean for my reply to come out sharp, but it does.

"And how many women have unwillingly married? How many innocents are we talking about here?" Jack's jaw sets and his eyes burn with fury. The dead tone from earlier replaced with a malice I wouldn't want directed at me.

"Twelve women already married when I left two days ago, several more up in the ceremony this weekend. They hold a ceremony with a minimum of three couplings every other week. Two in the last four months determined to be pregnant, but I'm not directly cleared for that information. What I hear is through the rumor mill, so there could be more. He's breeding nineteen year old kids, Jack, and no one can do a damn thing about it."

"How many total women are we talking about that would want to leave?"

"All of them. There are twenty seven women under the age of thirty at the compound and they're all scared. Most came in with their parents when they were kids. The older women would probably stay, the younger ones all want out. And almost thirty kids."

Jack lets out a low whistle. "I don't have that kind of housing, kid. Do you know what it would take to take care of that many people?"

My blood pumps loudly in my ears and I fist my hands in an effort to maintain my composure. "Make it happen, Jack. I know you took the company out from under my dad. I know it's a damn cash cow. I know you have the means."

"You misunderstand me. I didn't say I can't afford to set it up. I'm saying it's a hard ask for housing. Short from raising and maintaining funds to buy a literal apartment complex there's nowhere to go with that many people who have never lived anywhere on their own. You can't just integrate an entire doomsday compound throughout the city. And why do you think these fuckers all live together?" He points to Damien and James.

Damien nods his agreement. "It's not safe to be alone when you're talking about ex-mafia, man. They'll come looking for them and if they're split up, they're easier to take back."

"So, what do we do?" There has to be an answer. I won't leave here without one.

"Let me talk to Ginger, see what she knows."

"Ginger? The lady downstairs? Why would she know anything?"

Jack's grin grows into something almost sinister. "I'm sure you'll find out, pretty boy."

Damien's hand comes down on my shoulder as he laughs. "Welcome to the clubhouse. She's going to eat you alive."

CHAPTER THREE

Ginger

"How long did ya know somethin' like this was goin' on, Jack? You been sittin' on this and didn't say nothin'?"

He reels back like I slapped him, and I almost could. Cousins showing up unannounced at my counter, that have no business being as beautiful as they are, telling us things that shouldn't be ignored but apparently are. After everything we've worked on together. These are not acceptable situations and I'm beyond surprised.

"I always knew the situation could take a turn, but I swear, I had no idea my father had taken this drastic of an approach." Jack looks to Damien as if he needs him to confirm. They share a brief but silent conversation I wish I could be a part of, even once, and then Damien's attention returns to me.

"Russell always had the potential. He always made the fact that we had fewer fresh recruits and no new family bonds and his frustration with it known. But as of five years ago, forcing people to marry one another wasn't a discussion being had." He crosses his arms with finality, and I realize something.

"Why didja leave, Damien?"

"I thought we didn't need to talk about that."

"That was then, when I thought women was there of their own free will, not because someone says they get to stay and knock out some babies. This is now when I wanna know what's happenin' behind the walls yous guys are askin' me ta help empty. I think I got a right ta know now, don't you?" I match his stance with my arms firmly crossed over each other and a hip cocked. Dane looks between us, fascinated and slightly shrunk in like the awe only extends so far before the bit of fear or unease sets in.

"Teaching little kids to shoot first and ask questions later just isn't my thing, Ginger, and neither is feeding misinformation to people and invoking chaos to try to cause the very fall of a society you're building a compound to protect you from. It's lunacy. I was forced into a community I didn't want to be part of simply because I was born there. When I came of age, I should've had a choice to stay, but that's not how Russell runs things." The man I thought to be unshakable lets out an uneven breath and looks to the ceiling as though he's fighting tears before he sniffs and gives his shaggy hair a shake.

"I get that. I was born into somethin' I was stuck in, too. That's why I made this place. That's why I do so much ta help all of yous," I admit. I don't like to talk about my upbringing, the things I didn't get to say no to. "So, what are yous all proposing we do? Yer big, strong men. I'm not understandin' why ya need my help."

"We can get them out with a team just fine. We need somewhere for them to all go, Red." I glance at Dane, taking in his easy posture. "For some reason, these guys think you're the key to that."

"What, like a safe house?"

Jack looks at me intently. "Remember a few years ago when that guy offered you the apartment building a few blocks up for information about what his wife was doing here?"

"Yeah. What's he got ta do with it? I'm not givin' nobody no info about my patrons. I don't care who they think they are."

"The lot is empty. Not for sale even, just empty, and going to one of Troy's fundraiser auctions. But the auction is this Friday and it's invite only. My guess is that he found out about his wife and things went south. I was hoping you could find yourself an invite to that auction so I can buy it."

"You wanna house the women? You know how risky that is? Ya know he's gonna come lookin' here first. He ain't dumb, just like you."

"I'm not underestimating him. He'd never figure we'd keep them so close. And James knows some guys that could use some work, so I have a security team already put together ready to come the same day we tell them to. I have to do something, Ginger. Where else am I going to find a whole building so they can stay together?"

It's a massive risk, and I'm not convinced it'll blow over well. If Russell sends a team into the city, it'll be easy to find them once they come sniffing around Jack's. His house being so close to the club is a good thing for work, but not great when he's talking about moving escaped women and children only a few more blocks down. And yet–

"I'ma need a date, and it can't be either of yous, he'll recognize the two of yous if he's there. It'll mess things up."

Simultaneously the men turn to Dane who looks between them. "I'm guessing I won't like this."

"Got a tux, handsome?" He swivels to me and gives me a long look head to toe that makes my stomach do a little somersault.

"I'm sure I can find one somewhere. What do you have in mind, Red?"

The name makes my stomach spin again, his eyes seem to darken as he grins. I swallow to control my face and pull my shoulders back, buttoning up both the lust and the irritation. "Jackie baby, I think maybe I'll teach yer little cousin how to be a man. Any objections?"

His answer is a low chuckle before he turns to the doorway. Dane looks from Damien to the door where Jack disappeared, intrigue bringing his eyebrows up a bit while the rest of his face remains neutral.

"I told you, man; Ginger's gonna eat you alive. Good luck." And with that, the room is cleared save for Dane standing a few paces before me.

"I'll get one of the guys ta scrounge up a tux for ya, I think there's a few yer size. Do ya dance?"

His eyebrows shift together, and his head gives a little shake, his wavy hair giving a little bounce. "What?"

"Are ya' off somewheres else in yer head, or just purposefully obtuse? I gotta know now so's I know how much of a role I can actually give ya at the auction. So, ya tell me if ya can follow a conversation decently, then if ya can dance. Got it?" I could be poking a two hundred and fifty pound bear right in the chest with my attitude, but I need to gauge him. His walls are a mile high and made of the thickest steel around. He wears the info ticket for it right on his face in big bold letters that say, 'Stay Away'.

He takes a step forward, getting in my space. His face shutters impossibly further as he leans down closer to my level. Those deep blue eyes of his grow darker as he focuses completely on me. "I'm not sure what you usually get away with, but I will not tolerate insolence regardless of who is running the little show you're all planning."

"Oh, somebody is a big boy after all. Ya still didn't answer my question." I take a step closer, the toes of my shoes touching his. Intimidation won't work on me, but it'll be fun to watch him try.

Dane's hand comes up and cups the side of my jaw, his long fingers wrapping around my neck under my hair. His thumb is laying just under my chin, and he pushes it up. His eyes stay glued to mine as he firms his hold and his other hand comes to my waist before he gives a little push. His feet follow mine as he pushes me backwards, his hands pressing me sideways, then backward again in a simple fox trot. He jerks me into his firm body, tugging on my hair so my eyes meet his again and sweeps me to the side in a promenade before he twirls us effortlessly and then dips me. Dane follows me down and sweeps his nose up the column of my neck. Goosebumps break out across my shoulders and my breathing turns shallow, waiting for him to move.

Time feels like it's glitched and we're stuck here, his breath in my ear, mine barely dragging out of my lungs. Then he inhales sharply with a low noise in his throat and pulls me up. His hands grab my own and he turns us out to the left for two steps before returning to the right for two steps. He turns my hand to face me to a crowd that doesn't exist. When he turns us back to each other, he pulls me into his chest again, his lips to my ear.

"I trust you'll notify me when my tux arrives."

Dane abruptly shoves away from me and leaves through the still open doorway. I stand there in the middle of the room, taken completely by surprise, as I stare at the space he retreated through.

CHAPTER FOUR

Dane

It's two a.m. and I'm lying wide awake listening to someone down the hall snore. I've already been on my side with a pillow pressed into my ear twice, to no avail. I had my own cabin at the compound, I never let women stay the night, and my siblings are all at least ten years older than me, closer to Jack's age than my own. This is not something I've ever had to deal with.

Realizing my inner complaints make me sound like a spoiled asshole, I opt instead to get up and do something. I make my way in the dark to the kitchen and pop open the fridge for the pitcher of water I saw earlier.

"Didn't figure ya' for a boxer brief kinda guy but I will say it paints a pretty picture anyways."

I'm frozen for a moment trying to decide if I imagined her accent and that husky tone in her voice. I stand straight again and turn around to find Ginger sitting at the coffee table in the living room, a stack of paperwork in front of her and a little reading light illuminating them.

"Why are you in the dark, Red?"

She scowls at me, and I do my best to control the smile trying to creep up my cheeks.

"The name is Ginger, doll. And it's already a nickname so I don't need yous tryin'a gimme a new one. Red is ridiculous."

"Ginger is just another word for red, Red."

She crosses her arms over her chest, and I set the pitcher on the counter as I slowly pass it on my way to her. As I approach, her face turns stony, but she leans toward me slightly. I'm trained to read a person, and Ginger is clearly at war with something inside of her.

"This hair is burnt orange, doll. Red isn't orange, pumpkin, it's red."

I reach forward and grab a strand of her long locks where it's pulled loose from the messy bun she piled on her head, rubbing the strands between my fingers. She stills, her gorgeous green eyes peering up at me while she assesses my movements. "Huh. I suppose you're right, it does look orange, Red."

She swats my hand away and scowls at me again, breaking eye contact when I answer with a grin. Ginger focuses her full attention back on the papers in front of her.

Giving up for the moment, I plant myself in the seat next to her.

"What're you working on?"

She doesn't look at me, she just keeps shuffling papers and taking notes. "End of day."

"And what is end of day?" I ask, picking a page up. She snatches it back out of my hand with a huff.

"Confidential." The word comes out in a firm tone, her lips pursed together and her eyes leaving no room for argument.

I put my hands up in surrender. I'm not a fool, I know when I've pushed. She stares at me a moment and then turns back to her pile.

"What is it you do downstairs anyway?"

Ginger sighs heavily and rubs her eyes. "How much do yous guys know about Jack outside of his life with ya?"

"I can't speak for everyone, but I know he bought Adrian's business not too long ago. I know our dads weren't too pleased about it since my uncle set that business up for Adrian when he was young and it was not only a major source of income supporting the entire compound, but also our source of weapons. That shit is going to come back to bite him." And it will. It's only a matter of time. Him buying Adrian's life's work is what gave me a starting point in looking for him in the first place.

"All that sufferin' fer nothin'. You really know nothin'?" I shake my head, and she sighs again. "I run what is essentially an escort service. Too many women are on those phone apps takin' too many chances with men that don't answer ta nobody. So, they call me, tell me what they're lookin' fer, how the man needs ta be presented, and I send somebody out. Used ta just be normal dates, little things here and there. But then Jackie boy, he says lots of these women need ta know how ta be loved, right? What ta look fer next when they's done with us. How ta find happily ever after. And I thought that was a brilliant idea. So now we still sendin' out dates, but my men are busy buildin' women up instead of just winin' and dinin' em or bein' pretty arm candy."

"So, you're telling me you, what? Arrange services?"

"Not the way yous just said it, I don't! This is a classy joint, kid. And legal too. My men are brought in fer safe alternatives. They go ta business dinners and charity events and weddings with women who're worried about bein' taken advantage of. And rightfully so. Ya know how hard it is ta meet an honest man these days? 'Specially when yous got money and ya just need a date for somethin'?"

I shake my head slowly, not sure about the territory I just landed myself in.

"That because ya been livin' under that rock, or because ya just don't pay no attention?"

My lip curls, my anger suddenly presenting itself. I swallow it down before I speak, reminding myself she only knows what Jack has told her, and I don't know how much that is. "I didn't ask to live in that compound. And I imagine the women you meet are experiencing the same kind of fear the women in the compound are, never knowing who to trust. That's why I'm here."

The irritated look she was wearing slowly melts away before her head drops, looking to her hands that are now tangled together. "We all got a story, Dane. I wanna help yous give those women a better one."

I slide closer to her on the couch and push her chin up to meet my eyes. "I appreciate that. Help me understand how we can do that."

"If I clued ya in, it wouldn't be believable when the show starts." She grins at me, a grin laced with mischief and intention. I catch a small glint of her teeth through her lips and then her eyes close and she turns her head back to her paperwork and the bit of curiosity starting in me breaks.

"And why, again, can't your guys be in on this?"

"Because everyone knows 'em. This auction is gonna be high end players and their mugs've been all over this town at events just like this one, everyone'll know somethin's up. Yer fresh meat, beautiful, you'll do well."

"Why do I not like the sound of that?"

Ginger's attention comes back to me. "Because you seem like the bossy type. I'll let ya in on a little secret though; I'm in charge. And don't forget it."

I'm rendered speechless as I tangle myself in her intense stare. She's challenging me, refusing to break eye contact. I tilt my head, assessing her. Her eyebrows shoot up and I can't help the grin that breaks over my face.

"Oh, sweetheart, I wouldn't have it any other way." I back up from her, laying back into the couch and resting my hands behind my head. "I love a strong woman in charge. You go ahead and do what you want."

Ginger gives me an incredulous look before her features soften, her eyes hooding and her body language opening. She pulls her feet up off the floor to come to her knees on the couch, taking a few steps on them to where I'm sitting. When she leans in, I catch a whiff of the sweet perfume she's wearing and lick my lips. I wonder if she tastes as sweet as she smells.

She drags her pointer finger down my cheek and around the line of my jaw, drawing it to my lips before she stops and pulls the bottom one down slightly. She leans in, her face coming a breath away from my own and pauses.

Our air mingles together as this stunning specimen hovers just before me.

"And what do ya think I wanna do, Dane? Hm?" Her voice is soft and her gaze travels down my body, my torso bare, the bulge in my briefs visible, my legs spread out and bare as well. "The bigger question though is if yous got what it takes, big boy?"

Her tongue darts out and she licks my upper lip before patting me on the cheek several times with a laugh. Ginger stands from the couch and walks away from me without looking back.

Damn.

CHAPTER FIVE

Dane

Friday rolls around and I feel like I'm going out of my mind. I'm stuck in this apartment, having idle conversations with the various men that come and go, only ever spotting Ginger in the evenings long after everyone else has gone to sleep. She engages in my banter and then always leaves me shocked at her exit. In the time between, I learn that five other guys live here but it's a sort of between space for everyone downstairs to hang out when they aren't occupied.

Three of the five men that live here work for Ginger and they never stop talking; either about her or the women they've met this week. They bounce ideas off one another about how to best get them to open up, to trust them, to come out of their shell, to boost their self-esteem, the list goes on.

It's during one of these conversations that Alex, another of Jack's circle of men he came back to the compound to get out, barges through the apartment door. The door banging the wall in the entrance interrupts two of the men practicing a complicated ballroom dance together, trying to get ready for a dual assignment this weekend. Alex's face breaks into a huge smile, his shoulders rumbling slightly before he motions behind me to the hallway. He has a garment bag in his hand that I can only assume is the tux he took away the day prior for alterations.

"What exactly am I expecting?" I ask when he clicks the door closed and hangs the bag on the back of it.

"I've been advised you're not to be told a thing. Also, that you already know that." He pulls the zip on the bag down with a chuckle and pulls the tux over it. "Stay close to Ginger. You need to appear to be together, so treat her like she's yours and not the other way around."

"I'm not hers."

Alex pins me with a stare as I pull off my pants, his eyebrows lift. "In case you haven't noticed, everyone in this place belongs to Ginger. Give it a bit, you will, too."

"Yeah, I don't really get the whole Ginger high thing, but I'll let you know again next week how not into her I am. The woman seems pretty self-righteous if you ask me. Thanks for the help and all but that ego is something else entirely."

"She's been through it, man. You know she built all this from a run down, grungy sex shop to something high end all by herself, when she was only twenty, after escaping sex trafficking herself? If you can't look at that woman and watch what she does as she saves people in so many different ways and want to kiss her feet, there's something seriously wrong with your eyes."

I can't muster more than a grunt as he shoves the pants at me, and I work my way through the rest of the attire. When I'm dressed and working the bowtie to death, Alex steps in and ties it for me, then steps back again and whistles. "You clean up great, Fitzpatrick."

"Just Dane."

He cocks his head to the side and regards me. "You and Jack aren't so different, you know?"

I don't want to be compared to him. We share a name and half a bloodline, but that's where it ends until he proves otherwise. Our fathers want to keep people in and control them. Jack wants to keep everything else in his life tucked away, including us. I can't forgive him yet for never coming back.

"That's what I hear." I turn to assess myself in the long mirror and am surprised by the reflection staring back at me. I've never had use for a tux, but I could get used to this.

A soft knock on the door makes Alex and I both turn toward it before the latch releases and Ginger's head pokes in. Her eyes go round when she spots me, her lips falling just slightly open. Her gaze travels up my body and she closes her lips again when she lands on the smug expression I can feel on my face. She clears her throat and steps in.

I'm stunned by the fiery red dress she's wearing, her shoulders completely bare and the bodice clinging to her breasts is the only thing holding it up. Her skin is creamy and dotted in light freckles enticing me to come closer and count them. I make my way back up her smooth, half bare legs to land on a low ponytail pulled over one shoulder, the ends of her curls splashing across her collarbone and her eyes darkened with deep blue shadow making her look sultry.

Ginger might look like an ordinary woman when you walk into her door, but every time I set eyes on her when the closing sign turns, she's like a succubus; enchanting, addicting without even one touch. And oh, what I wouldn't give to find out what that one touch could do to me. Realizing I've been staring far too long, I echo Ginger's sentiment and clear my own throat of the gravel lodging itself there.

"Looks like Alex got ya all done up, doll. Ya ready ta go get us a complex?" She folds her hands in front of her and looks up at me through her lashes.

"Still wish I knew how exactly we're going to manage that. Beyond that I am." Stepping forward, I offer her my arm and open the door, escorting her through it.

Cat calls ring through the common space in the apartment on our way to the door. Ginger grins and blushes slightly, laughing when they turn their attention to me. She grabs a small handbag off a hook next to the door as I open it. I flip the room the bird when she's made her way to the stairs, closing the door behind me.

I follow Ginger out onto the street where she's already working on hailing a cab. "This works one way, Dane Fitzpatrick, and one way only. Yer new last name is Franklin courtesy of one Miss Ellen Franklin, Mrs. Ellen Fitzpatrick now. You can thank her when ya meet her. One hell of a woman, that one."

A cab pulls up and Ginger sprints for the door, climbing inside and sliding all the way over. I realize I'm being awkward again, standing here looking over the vehicle so I climb in after her.

Ginger turns to me after prattling off an address to the driver. "How old are you, handsome?"

"Twenty three."

She lets out a low whistle. "Hot damn, I'd have never guessed that low. And I've been doin' this a long time. Yous thirty two now and ya reside at what's technically

Jack's office but'll do in a pinch like this. Nobody's gonna check. Memorize this." I take the ID from her hand and look it over.

"Oddly enough, that's almost right."

"What is, sugar?"

I flip the ID around and hold it out, pointing to the birth date. "Franklin's birthday is July 5th, mine's the 6th. Almost right."

"Well done, Ellen." She grins a cat-like grin and holds up two fingers. "Second; you are not ta leave my side all night unless I say, ya hear me? Third; make sure you win. No limits." She hands me a black card with Jack's name on it and gives me a firm nod. "I mean it."

"What am I bidding on?" Curiosity has the best of me. If we're looking to win the apartment complex, surely Jack's card isn't something we should be using.

"You'll know." Is all she says before she pulls a compact out of her bag and checks her hair. As cool and collected as she is, there's an underlying air of nervousness. She's keeping it buttoned tight, but I can see it there in the subtle wiggle of her toes, like she's resisting bouncing her whole leg. She runs her fingers over the outline of her cherry red lips repeatedly despite there being nothing there and then pops them as the compact snaps shut.

If I didn't know it before, I do now; we're walking into something bigger than just charity. The question is what that is, exactly.

CHAPTER SIX

Ginger

We walk into the ballroom and my nerves are as big a bundle as the mile high ceilings in this place. The smooth white surface is brushed in swirls that almost give it a cloud appearance before moving down into barely peach-colored walls with ornate pillars. Swanky.

My eyes sweep the room as we move deeper into it. It looks like a full house tonight with clusters of people around what is maybe a dozen high top tables and in the larger open space in front of the stage, packed in like a mosh pit waiting for a show to start. But as I take another look, I don't see any heavy pockets among any of the groups of people. Winning among this crowd is never a problem, they all like to talk a big game but cheap out unless something is absolutely worth the trouble. That's why the deal for the apartments has me concerned.

Idle chatter is happening all around us and it's not too long before I'm roped into a conversation. Much to my satisfaction, Dane stays right where I told him to; by my side. A man like that, raised to be an obedient soldier, I guess I shouldn't have doubted he'd listen. My stomach warms at the thought of how far his obedience might go but I shake it off. This is not the time, nor the place and he could almost be my kid. But his hand keeps rubbing the inside of my upper arm as he stands stock still like a beautiful statue and listens politely to people prattle about nonsense. And he smells amazing.

It was more than slightly shocking to walk into that room earlier and see him standing there in Jack's old tux, looking very much like the Jack I first met all those years ago. I loved that boy with everything that was in me, beautiful Jack and his soulful eyes and his tattered heart. As stunning and as kind of a creature as Jack is though, he never stirred me like Dane's presence has. They have the same dark hair, the same broad shoulders, the same no-nonsense glare. But where Jack's eyes are a smooth green and gold that seemingly match with his nearly black locks, Dane's are a startling blue that seem surreal with such dark hair. The light here makes them more vibrant than the low lighting I've seen him in all week, and I can't stop sneaking a glance while I take in the bergamot radiating off of him.

"–interested in seeing what happens in your neck of the woods." Mr. Donaldson is staring at me, waiting for a reply to whatever he was saying. I open my mouth to draw the inquiry back to him to see if I can get him to ask again but I'm cut off.

"The area is certainly expanding. We're all on the edge of our seats waiting to see what developments might pop up." Dane smiles politely and gives my arm a squeeze as he finishes.

"Yes, that's right. Very excitin' time it is." I still have no idea what he was talking about, as distracted as I was. I need to shake the charm flowing from Dane's skin touching my own. Good save though.

A glass clinks several times and the room quiets as everyone swivels to follow the sound to the stage. Troy Richards stands on stage with his champagne flute in one hand and a spoon in the other. Crazy asshole wouldn't even care if that thing broke considering he owns half of the condos uptown, and his foundation is the one running this show tonight. I personally know these flutes each cost as much as I bring in with an entire day of appointments, since I broke one two years ago and got billed for it.

"Gracious guests, welcome back to our foundation fundraiser auction. If you're here you know why, if you don't you should ask your neighbor. We thank you once again for joining us for exclusive access to many of our city's treasures. We're so glad we could hold them hostage for you." He grins and the room fills with quiet laughter. The nerve of this snarky asshole. "We'll keep the champagne flowing while you keep your checkbooks flowing in return. Remember, your contributions keep our streets safer."

"Yeah, from yous," I mutter under my breath, irritated. But Dane doesn't miss it. His brows draw together as he looks from me and back up to the stage.

Troy steps back as the applause begins and the auctioneer steps up to the podium in his place. The stage curtain pulls back and reveals a beautiful painting. I don't know anything about art and don't bother following along. We have our card tonight for one thing and one thing only.

The painting sells for a pretty penny, as does the tennis ball sized sapphire necklace and earring set. Troy is standing on the sidelines looking increasingly annoyed about the vase collection and Civil War era antiques that barely bring in anything. Until his gaze catches on me. The curve of his lips is probably meant to look like a grin, but it's vile. I snap my attention back to the podium where photos of a house are being displayed. The first of many properties being auctioned tonight.

Troy's game is rather simple. He sells properties at ridiculous prices to folks who can't afford them but want out of the dangerous, crowded parts of town. Then he jacks up interest sky high on the loans he personally offers them.

Within eight years, folks can't afford the loans anymore and have to fold on them.

Then he brings the properties to bid on at these auctions and sells them for an asinine amount of money all in the name of 'keeping our streets safe' through his gated services. Bidders get rights to security at locations they've purchased as well, for the first five years. Trouble is, he doesn't bother telling anyone it's his thugs that run the streets to begin with. No, you find that out from knowing people on the inside. A fact that's only just barely protected my business; because some of those inside men work for me.

My palms feel damp as the auction numbers click down. Thirty items up for auction tonight, and Troy runs them as a countdown. The number one item is the item he deems most valuable for the evening. Tonight, that was supposed to be the complex we're here to win.

Item two on the docket is called; a microbrewery that's in need of repair and most of its equipment needing replacing, but had a good following before they folded. There's a restaurant attached to one side with an open floor plan and a separate club upstairs.

I turn to Dane. "Remember, doll, whatever it takes. There ain't no limit on that card." I pop up on my toes and brush my lips over his cheek. He looks at me with clear confusion on his face as I walk away.

I make it not two steps before his fingers are circling my wrist. "What the hell, Red?"

"No limit," I repeat and pull my wrist free.

The microbrewery sells for just over a million and I sigh, hoping like hell that the lowball price was because no one wanted to tackle the project of fixing it up, and not that it's going to be a cheap night for the big ticket items. That property is in a hot part of the city and should have pulled in two million with the security contract, easy.

"And the last item on tonight's list. Oh, ladies and gentlemen, I'm very excited about this one! It looks like we have had a bit of a change in agenda tonight. The last item on our list is something special indeed. Ginger's has been known to grace us with donations of her handsome gentleman's time but tonight, Ginger herself is offering five exclusive evenings as your escort with an open contract for any event. Her most exclusive gentlemen's prices begin at fifty thousand dollars per assignment, so let's open this bidding graciously doubled at five hundred thousand for five exclusive evenings."

I've made it to the center of the stage by the time he finishes introducing my "offer" of the evening. I was reluctant to accept this approach that Troy so vehemently insisted must be open contract. But it was the only way he would agree to my invitation, since he knew I wanted that building, it being the thing I'd asked for first. I simply wanted to buy it before auction and offer him another small store I owned further downtown. Troy, however, had wanted to book me for as long as I can remember, and I don't take contracts. Especially not with sadistic men like him.

My eyes move to find Dane in the crowd. He's moved forward but his look of surprise seems to have overtaken him. I nod to him, trying to break him out of his spell.

Two things have to happen here. First and foremost, he *cannot* let Troy win this thing. He isn't known to be a nice man behind closed doors, he breaks his toys, and having an open contract would make me just that; a toy. Second, he needs to keep Troy bidding. If I want the building, my bids have to skate over two million dollars, that was the agreement.

"–do I hear seven hundred and ninety thousand?"

Come on Dane. His eyes could burn a hole right through the heads of the men in front of him. His arms-crossed stance is rigid, his glare as icy and pissed off as it is hot and angry.

"Oh-ho thank you, Mr. Richards! Impressive indeed! Do I hear 1.2 million dollars for a five night open contract with Ginger herself? 1.2 million, anyone?"

The room stays silent, and I try hard to control my face, but my breathing won't slow down. Something in Dane's jaw ticks and his eyes narrow at me. The look is promising of the anger he'll surely have to rein in later. "One million seven hundred thousand," he bites out, his eyes not leaving me, his body not moving an inch.

The crowd of men in front of him turn to look.

"Mr. Richards, it seems you have a competitor. One million seven hundred thousand. Do I hear one million and eight?"

Dane arranges his features and coolly turns his head over his shoulder to look at Troy across the room, arms still crossed. I see an eyebrow cock in a dare. But Troy isn't as skilled at controlling his features. He looks visibly flustered and rightfully so. No one ever bids against him, and in this case, it's his arrangement. If he bids too much higher, he loses the building he wanted to keep, but if he doesn't continue, he loses his only chance at what he really wants; me.

"One million nine hundred," he offers.

"Two million." Dane doesn't even offer the auctioneer a chance to acknowledge Troy's bid.

Troy's arms uncross and he stands up straight off the high top he was leaning on. "Two million and five."

Dane's answer is a chuckle as the auctioneer reiterates the bid. Dane glances at me before he shakes his head returning to Troy, mirroring his posture. "Four. Four million."

A collective gasp sounds and everything goes still. Troy purses his lips and puts his hands in his pockets. He pauses for only a few seconds before he strolls over to Dane. "Who are you?" he asks, inches from Dane. Men come in off the walls to stand behind Troy. His head tilts, scrutinizing Dane, looking for any recognition.

"New in town, but I think I like it here. Miss Ginger here was kind enough to show me around. Of course, I can't miss an opportunity to get a bit of a private tour, if you catch my drift."

Troy's nostrils flare and his toes move to nudge Dane's. "How do we know you can meet a bid like that? This is a fundraiser for charity, we're not giving it away in this room."

Dane pulls the black card out of his pocket, holding it up between two fingers. "No limit," he repeats, snatching his hand back when Troy grabs for the card. "And I don't take kindly to intimidation. You didn't ask anyone else if they could afford their bids. Kindly attempt to outbid me or let the gentleman on the stage finish his job so I can pay for my prize."

"Four million, then. Go ahead Roger, four million." Troy breaks eye contact first, his fake smile reassuring for Roger, the auctioneer.

Roger looks shaken but manages to shutter out the confirmation. "Impressive indeed. Miss Ginger, I don't think we've ever seen a bid this high." He laughs unsteadily, then turns back, looking for another bid.

Dane is studying his nails, his confidence looking completely unrattled. "Four million five hundred thousand," he says, not even looking up.

"Four and seven," Troy fires back, astonishment clear on his face at Dane's audacity in outbidding himself.

"Six."

Troy's attention snaps to the doorway in the back of the room. One of the guys stationed there touches the com in his ear. Roger calls once, twice, the man shakes his head and Troy throws up his hands, stalking to the window. He has one hand on his hip and the other in his hair when Roger calls the sale and applause roars through the room.

People are patting Dane on the back as he signs the contract and I slowly come off stage, but I'm shook. I had no idea Troy would push so hard and now I can't help but wonder if we screwed ourselves in the process of trying to do good. On one hand, we lined Troy's pockets for the year and ensured added security for the building. On the other,

none of us are safe from his goons if he decides he's
exceptionally angry about being one upped in public.

CHAPTER SEVEN

Ginger

"What the hell, Ginger?" Dane's face is dark with anger while managing to maintain some sort of pleasant appearance to the people around us. It's a confusing combination.

"Oh, I'm Ginger now, am I? Look, you did good, kid."

"Don't fucking 'kid' me, Red. What was that?" His hand grips my elbow, his fingers firmly biting into my flesh.

I search his eyes. Adrenaline and something like fear swirl there. I can feel it swirling in me, too, but we need to be cool. "Not here."

Dane doesn't miss a beat as he stalks to the entryway, zigzagging around people as he tows me behind him. I scramble to match his pace; we're drawing too much attention. "Ya gotta slow down, I'm good in heels, but shit I'm not that good."

He answers me with a scowl. Looping my arm through his elbow, I give a tug and somehow manage to keep my balance without making a complete spectacle. Balance that requires a heavy hang on Dane's arm.

He searches me down to my toes. When his gaze drifts up to my face again, his eyebrows smooth out with an exhale. "Sorry."

I nod without waiting to see if he has more to say and finish our walk through the door out into a maze of hallways. The wing of this building is one I know well though, and it only takes a few turns before the hum of voices behind us dies away completely.

"Sit," I tell Dane as we approach a black leather chair against the ornate, cement walls. This building is meant to look classic, and expensive without actually being so. *Big wigs and their money.* What they do with it can't actually buy you class, but they sure try.

I swing my foot up on the armrest. "Buckle me?" My voice is soft, and his eyes travel up my bare calf, sweeping over my thigh and up my torso to land on my own eyes. His fingers trail my calf in the same manner, before pulling my foot closer to him so he can adjust the buckle that's still clasped.

"What is this game?" His voice is low but much calmer than it was a minute ago in the crowded, loud room.

"That's just it, doll, a game we all has ta play when our neighborhood is owned by the bad guys. Ya did good though. Saved me five very unpleasant evenin's."

"Says who?" Dane's grip tightens on my ankle. He puts it back where it landed to begin with and pushes my knee away. The dress I'm wearing slides with it, exposing my inner thigh and a direct path for Dane. I drop my knee onto the arm of the chair, drawing his eyes back up to meet mine. "It seems I've got an exclusive five evenings with you, dear Ginger. Bought and paid for."

"That's mine and Jack's money," I snap, slapping his hand away. The fiery trail his fingers left burns over my skin.

"Might be your money, but it's my name on the purchase, Red."

"You better watch yerself."

"Or what?" Dane grins at me as he leans forward into my space and my blood boils.

Coming around the front of the chair I take only a second to brace myself before planting one foot into Dane's chest and pushing him back against the chair. He grabs my calf and his grin grows. "Ya want those five nights? Yer gonna earn 'em. Six million dollars? I figure that's about a hundred assignments. Who you workin' for, baby? Me, or my list of ladies?"

Dane scoffs, a little laugh leaving him with it. "One hundred assignments for five nights? That hardly seems fair. Especially with the way you pulled me into that with no warning."

"First thing ya need ta know is how ta roll on the fly. Though I can't use ya in this crowd again since they all's know who ya are now thanks to that little tiff in there. The second thing ya need ta know is how ta speak to a lady, ya brat. Especially a lady that just put her own neck on the line for yous. And a cool mill of my own I might add. Gonna take me ages ta earn that back with Troy breathin' down my neck."

Dane pushes my foot off his chest and pulls my knee forward, toppling me into his lap. I'm half straddling the chair and leaning into him when his fingers grip my chin, and he comes inches away from me.

"First, it seems I only owe you about twenty assignments to make back your million." His eyes drop to my lips for a moment before he wets his own and his eyes travel back to mine. But I don't meet his gaze, my eyes are distracted by the glisten of his bottom lip, its fullness now reflecting in the low light over our heads.

"Second, I don't need a lesson in how to speak to a woman."

"A lady," I cut in, my entrancement interrupted.

"A lady. I give what I receive. You're wild and sharp and it's making me agitated. I want to strip you down and spank your ass until you apologize. And I don't need to speak differently to you to accomplish that."

His mouth snaps shut and his nostrils flare. I feel my eyebrows arch before I compose my face, swallowing while I collect myself because if I don't, I'll find myself doing something beyond stupid when we have a lot of work left to do.

"Well then. Maybe there's more work ta do than I originally thought. Let's go collect that card and the keys and see what we're walkin' into, huh?" I can't bring myself to move, locked in the intensity raging behind his eyes. My heart ticks up for several beats before I will myself to stand straight and pull my dress down, smoothing my hands over my thighs in an attempt to keep my resolve from cracking. There's energy practically crackling in the air, and his threat echoes through me.

Dane clears his throat and takes a deep breath before he rises from the chair and not so subtly adjusts himself. He flashes me a megawatt, fake ass smile with a little head shake and holds his hand out signaling me to lead the way. I take the hint and start walking down the hall, looking back once and catching him watching my ass as we go.

CHAPTER EIGHT

Dane

"How pissed, exactly, is Jack going to be that we spent five million dollars of his money, and this place needs probably half a million more in work before we can say go? And in two days? Isn't that a premium or something?"

Ginger is silent, shaking her head as she continues walking through the apartment we're in muttering something under her breath about a rat-faced asshole. Her gasp when we walked in spoke enough volumes and she hasn't said a word while inspecting broken doors, burned floors, and the mounds and mounds of trash and human waste everywhere.

We finish looking at the entire first floor and head up oddly pristine stairs to the second floor, only to find bags of garbage torn open as soon as we come off the landing, their contents rotting on the hallway floors and in front of the doors.

I hear her speak before I turn around. "Jackie baby? Ya need to come down here pronto. Bring James and the boys, and lots of trash bags. Call Phil, get the biggest dumpster he has available and make sure his crew is up before the sun. We ain't got no time for this." She's somber when she hangs up the phone.

"It's going—"

"Don't. Don't say 'It's gonna be okay, Red'. Just don't. This is a lotta work and we ain't got enough guys for it. I'ma have ta call in more favors ta get more men down here just ta clean out this literal trash pile. I thought we was just gonna have ta come in here and clean out cobwebs, wash some floors, maybe give it a fresh coat of paint so's we can bring in some furniture. But this? Who the fuck does this?!"

She's fuming, her posture rigid, and then she does something I never would have expected. She growls, letting out her pent-up anger and punches the wall.

"Ugh! Fuck!" Ginger pulls her hand back, shaking it and hissing. I clear the distance between us in just a few quick strides, despite how far away she was, pulling my hands out of my pockets so I can look at hers.

"Why do yous men do that all the time? That hurts!" She hisses again when I move her third finger.

"Well, it's not broken. All those big, burly men around and none of them ever taught you how to throw a punch so you didn't break or dislocate anything?"

She throws an irritated look at me, her lips closed, and I catch her other hand as she whips it around, clearly aiming for the back of my head. I can't help the chuckle that leaves me as I bring the hand to my mouth and give it a kiss before relinquishing it to her.

"Easy, Red. Don't want to hurt that one, too. This one though. This one is just going to hurt like hell for a bit."

"What're we gonna do, Dane?" Her eyes are glistening, threatening tears at me.

"You're asking me? I thought you were in charge, beautiful. So, you tell me. What's next?"

Her eyes search mine, now welling with tears. She looks down and lets out a sound between a laugh and a sob. "Nuthin. Do you know how much this dress costs?" Ginger erupts into laughter, moving back a step.

I watch her with amusement until she calms, sighing. "Come on then, let's go get changed so we can come back and get started. It's going to be a long night."

***

The first thing I notice when we get out of the cab is that it seems unnaturally dark on the street. Unnatural for the city, anyway. This is the sort of dark I'm accustomed to at home, away from the light. Ginger is moving ahead of me, but I catch up and tug her back against my chest.

"What–"

"Shh." Looking up I see both the safety lights on the front of her building smashed out. The red light is on inside the first floor, but the hall light is out on the stairs heading up to the apartment over the business. We stand deathly still and wait. I don't like standing here in the open, but I need a sound to decide; any sound. *Come on, give us a hint.*

Glass breaks inside Ginger's and I have to decide what to do. Sending her into the hallway leading upstairs where there should be other people there to protect her, I pull the door to the business open wider so I can slide inside. I tuck myself into the shadows the deep red light helps create and move along the wall.

A grunt comes from the portal of black leading into the hallway then a thud. That was definitely a body against a wall. Flesh on flesh sounds before a roar of gusto and Vince the bodyguard comes flying through from the darkness. Following just behind him is a bald man. I recognize the tattoo on his forearm from the event we just caused a scene at. I press myself further into the wall, letting the shadows enclose around me as he stalks to the counter and breaks open locked drawers.

The man's head snaps up as the door swings open. "Oh my God, Vince!" Ginger rushes into the room and I curse silently to myself.

The man stalks to her as she squats down to check on Vince. His large frame engulfs her petite frame as he drags her up from behind, his big hands hooked in her elbows. Ginger gasps and kicks her legs up in the air as he hauls her backward several steps. I wait for the moment he moves just in front of me to jump out at him.

The suddenness of my attack surprises him and I wrap him in a choke hold. I don't know who this guy is, but he's nearly a foot taller than me and impossibly thick. I look around for something to grip with my legs or to use to my advantage to get higher because I only have seconds before he gets his own bearings and makes what's already a situation against my odds, even worse. With nothing in close enough proximity, I let my weight drop and hope he goes down easy.

Baldy wiggles, agitated, trying to hold on to Ginger who is putting up a hell of a fight up front while he also works to shake me off. He seems to slow until he takes a deep breath in, holds still for a heartbeat of a second and then turns Ginger and shoves her into the door frame. Her back and head hit with a deafening sound, and she cries out at the same time he braces his legs and flips me over his shoulders.

I land harshly on the ground beside him, sideways, and I'm pretty sure I feel a rib crack. The air sucks out of my lungs and I cough out a wheezing sound. A blade glints in baldy's hand, and he grins, his eyes zeroing back in on Ginger.

He takes a step toward her and all rational thought leaves me as I scramble to my feet, adrenaline winning out over the intense pain coming from my ribs. I throw myself over her as his blade comes down, slicing itself through the flesh over my hip.

Ginger screams and reaches a hand into her dress. Silver glimmers softly in the crimson light around us before my ears start ringing from the close range shot she fires over my shoulder. Baldy falls to the ground, his knife clattering against the floor. I press my eyes closed, moving off her and slump backward against the wall, willing my ear drums to chill the fuck out and slam a hand against my aching side. Ginger's cool hands disrupt the calm I'm trying to force my body into, and I open my eyes to find her face inches from my own.

"Shit! Dane! What'd you do that for, huh?" Ginger barks at me, clear irritation on her face, but her eyebrows are drawn like she's actually worried.

I pull my hand away, coated in blood and press it back down again. "Call it instinct."

"You coulda been killed!"

"Right back at ya, Red! Was that gun strapped to your thigh?"

"Of course it was. Ya think I'd go to an event where everybody in the room would shoot first and ask questions later without a gun?"

"Jesus. Do you roll with the mafia or something?"

"Somethin' like that," she replies.

"I was kidding," I say and I feel my face fall.

"Well, I ain't. When the only father figure in your life is your mom's pimp and the Johns comin' and goin' and she'd rather sell ya' to 'em than stop the flow of candy, a girlie learns some things. Now get yer ass up before the cops get here because I'm pretty sure yer daddy owns half the force and the other half will be here with Troy so yous shouldn't be."

James comes bursting through the open door, his eyes wild and starting to bruise, his hands bloody. He's breathing heavily as he rushes to Ginger.

"It's fine," she scolds, swatting his hands away. "Get Dane out of here. If there's more bodies upstairs, take him to Jack's. And get Jack over here. This ain't gonna be pretty."

CHAPTER NINE

Dane

A very irate Jack shoves me into a large bathroom before hurriedly introducing me to his wife, something I truly didn't expect, and steering James to the door. He looks the bigger man up and down with a grunt that James returns and they leave me here without another word.

"Do you want to tell me what happened?" Ellen lifts my shirt gingerly like she might hurt me more than the giant open wound in my side. Her hands are small and delicate but it's the round bump in her midsection I'm zoned in on. I worry, not for the first time, about the innocent people in Jack's life. The other lives we could implode in an idiotic effort to rescue other innocents that I just can't let go of. "Hey," she probes.

I shake my head and take a shuddering breath. "Sorry, got lost for a minute. I don't know what happened. There was a guy in Ginger's and he went for her, so I jumped in his way and well, this. No idea what it was about."

"I imagine Ginger was both grateful and angry with you." She's distracting me as she probes around at the wound. I don't ask how she knows what she's looking at. I don't want to know if she knows or is just guessing.

"I didn't have time to register if she was actually angry. In the moment it seemed like a better idea to get stabbed than to watch her get stabbed. I don't care if she's mad about it."

Her eyebrows rise as she presses a wet cloth to my wound. It burns and I do my best not to jump. "You might care tomorrow. She won't let you forget you got hurt for her, even if she is grateful. Ginger isn't one to take these things lightly."

"You sound like you have experience in that."

"I have ears and spend enough time with men who like to talk." Ellen picks up a spray bottle and apologizes at the same moment it streams over the wound. The liquid burns through the cut and makes it feel like I'm being stabbed all over again.

The searing pain makes me jump in my seat, trying and failing to back up. Ellen holds my legs steady as she watches the wound while she sprays it again. "Damnit, woman!"

"I did say sorry." Her eyes are sincere if not slightly mischievous. I eye her belly again and decide to distract myself.

"What do you have going on in there?"

She looks puzzled for a moment before following my gaze. A soft smile works her lips, and she touches the round front with her other hand. "A little girl. We didn't expect her but that's okay. Do you have any kids, Dane?"

My answer is immediate. "No. I'd never want to raise any in the compound."

"Ah yes, that. You know Jack and I have been having a lot of discussions about that the last few days. He has a pretty solid plan. I hope you two can see past all the ghosts to really make this work. He has a story, too, you know."

I don't have an answer for her, so I watch her nimble hands work to stitch up my side instead. Whatever she sprayed on me was clearly to clean it, but it numbed the skin as well and I'm glad for it. When she's finished and cuts off the excess floss, she runs her hand over my ribs where a deep purple ring is starting to surface.

"These don't look good. I don't know what I can do about that. You may need to go see someone." Her voice is apologetic, but it's unnecessary.

"I've cracked a rib or two in my time, it'll be fine. Thanks for stitching me up, doc."

"I'm a florist." She laughs.

"Not tonight you're not."

Ellen smiles at me and turns around as the door downstairs closes. She hands me a clean shirt and a pair of sweatpants. Jack makes his way through the bathroom door as I'm pulling the hem of my shirt in place.

"What's the verdict?" he asks and pulls Ellen into his side before placing a kiss on her head.

"I think he'll live." She grins and winks at me.

Jack's eyes skate my way and he crosses his arms, back to the authoritative figure. "I think we should wait a few days before we take the compound."

"What? You can't be serious. We've already waited a whole damn week. Tonight was a win; we got the apartments. We agreed on tomorrow night." I bolt to my feet, ignoring the burning protest of the fresh stitches.

"In case you didn't notice, kid, you basically got stabbed. The guy upstairs was a compound guard, the guy Ginger shot was one of Troy's. Both parties are mad and seem to know each other. It makes me wonder exactly how much of what goes on around here they're aware of back home that clearly, you don't know about." Jack's eyebrow raises as he challenges me to argue with him. I scoff and turn to the sink, running the water cold to scoop it over my face.

"Look, I'm not saying we don't go. I'm saying we skip town for a few days, take eyes off us, then go in when they think we've run away with our tails between our legs. The teams will still be here working on the building."

It's a solid plan, to let them get distracted either by something else or trying to figure out where we went. And it takes a possible mole or bug out of the equation. If the neighborhood thug was in cahoots with our parents, we had more issues to deal with than we thought; more kings on the board than we need to eliminate safely.

"I'm not saying you're right; I'm just saying that your plan isn't wrong."

Jack turns to Ellen and places another kiss on her head. "Go pack a bag, beautiful."

Two short hours later, as the sun moves high into the sky, Vince, James, Ginger and I are in the back of a black SUV as Jack winds us up hills less than twenty miles from the compound with Ellen in the passenger seat. He owns a ski resort back here, apparently, and there's a large private cabin on the back of the grounds. Headquarters, he said.

After a quick perimeter sweep, Jack and Ellen have gone to their room, Vince was ordered to lay down and nurse his concussion, and James, Ginger and I are sitting around a coffee table in front of a fire in complete silence.

"Why only two men?" Ginger asks after her second glass of wine. Her eyes are glued to the fire, her voice void of any indication of what she's feeling. "I just don't get it. There's no less than ten of yous guys in that building at any time and they only send in two men?"

"It was just a spook, Ginger. It was late on a Friday night. I don't think they were expecting anyone to be around or awake. The only reason the guy upstairs got through so many men is because so many were already asleep or not expecting anything." James takes an audible swallow of his whisky, exhaling just as loudly and looks at her seriously. "They were looking for you though, babe. No more sleeping at the club. At least for now."

Her face finally turns to his. "I ain't no coward."

"Didn't say you were. But you're more of a liability to the men if they're concerned with protecting you as well as themselves."

"Who's the boss here, huh?"

James huffs out a single, shallow laugh. "If I can't be bossy occasionally, then what the hell do you pay me for, Ginger?"

She makes a soft noise in her throat and stares down into her glass with a sigh. She shocks the living hell out of me when she puts it on the table and tucks her feet under herself before she lays her head on my lap and pulls a blanket over her legs.

I look at James, but he shrugs and finishes his drink, leaving his own glass next to Ginger's. He looks at me for a moment and then walks towards the bedrooms, squeezing my shoulder as he passes. My fingers itch to dig into her hair as it shines brightly in the fire in front of us. My heart kicks up a notch thinking about how it might feel wrapped between my fingers, and I give up, slowly sinking into it to massage her scalp.

Ginger makes a sleepy noise that's almost like a moan and I brush my hand through the length, savoring the silky slide against my skin. The repetitive motion soothes the nerves still screaming inside me and my eyes get heavy.

The next thing I know, Jack is shaking me awake. I startle out of sleep, a weight still in my lap and Jack's fingers move to his lips as he points to Ginger draped delicately over my legs. He nods toward the kitchen, and I carefully work myself out from under her.

In the kitchen, Jack hands me a glass of water and some pain relievers. "How's that wound?"

"It's there. I'll survive."

"I sure hope so because we need to start prepping to move out, in about an hour."

I'm sure my head shake is a good show of how shocked I am considering the way Jack's arms cross as he leans on the counter. "Not that I'm not grateful for the acceleration but, what changed?"

"I still have eyes in the compound. It's not easy getting any word from inside, but it's easier when we're here. We spooked them earlier just as much as they spooked us, they're locking down, getting ready to move everyone underground. If they put everyone in that vault instead of just family heads, we're not getting anyone out."

There's a quiet knock on the door and Jack walks across the space to open it. A man comes in dressed in tactical gear pushing a cart full of silver covered plates. He stands up straight and pushes up his visor. "Dinner is served," Alex announces with a smile.

CHAPTER TEN

Dane

In the next twenty minutes everyone is awake and eating as an entire team of men flood in. I had no idea Jack has a team like this, and I can only hope it's a well-hidden fact from more than just me. Damien arrives and passes out more gear and as soon as my plate is empty, I'm dressed and strapping padding to my body and weapons in my holsters. I'm as impressed with the quality of the material and the array of weapons I'm handed as I am hopeful, I won't have to use all of them.

When I return to the kitchen, the island has been cleared of dishes and maps are being poured over. Several conversations are happening at once among small clusters of men. My eye catches on a flash of red in the corner and I look over to find Ellen helping Ginger strap a chest piece across her shoulders.

"No," I say, stalking that way. I don't need to see the maps; I know that place like the curve of my cock.

"Good morning to you, too, doll." Ginger speaks but ignores me, tightening a glove over her injured hand instead.

"You're not going in."

"Says who? Yer not the boss of me."

"What are we, like eight?"

"Doesn't matter. I'm goin' in ta help pull them kids out. Ain't enough people otherwise. Ellen'd come, too, but–" She gestures at Ellen's stomach. "So, finish packin' up, buttercup, and do try ta be a good boy and listen, hm?"

"Who has lead on the women's barracks?" I ask over my shoulder to no one in particular.

"You," Damien pipes up as Ginger grins at me. That has my attention enough to spin around.

"You need me to get inside."

"We sure don't," Jack disagrees. "We need you to make sure everyone you want us to go in for, gets out. None of us have been there for at least half a decade. And no one was there last week when you had a head count on people who wanted out. You go in with Ginger, James and their team through the drain tunnels and make sure no one is missed. Besides, it makes more sense to have a woman with you. Men are the ones in this place trying to control them. Ginger is good with shit like that."

She beams me another smile and it rattles me, making my dick jump while I push down my irritation at the fact that Jack's right. "And where will everyone else be?"

Damien's arm slings over my shoulder and he leans on me casually. "Keeping everyone else busy so they don't notice the five white vans, two short buses and the little people running around, of course."

"Some of the men are only on guard duty because they have to be and are otherwise innocent."

"We're shooting non-lethals tonight, kid. They'll hurt like hell but won't kill anyone."

Well shit, looks like Jack thought ahead on everything. Someone outside honks twice and Jack rolls the maps up off the island. "That's it, guys. Stay with your partner, silent calls only, and make sure you both come back in one piece. No one gets left behind."

"Yer my partner, doll," Ginger says, slipping her arm through mine.

"What the hell is a silent call?"

"These." Alex hands me earpieces. "There's a button on each. Press it and it'll communicate directional instructions to your partner without you needing to speak. We're planning on total darkness, it's helpful with the night vision sets. Rapid click either side twice and it'll send an alert to everyone that there's trouble. Try not to freak everyone out, okay?"

James and Damien each pat me on the back as they brush past me while I'm placing the earpieces. I click the button on my left side and Ginger turns, holding up her left hand. She clicks the button in her ear and a soft computer voice says 'right'.

"Interesting."

"They develop a lot of unique gear in the ivory tower, as you like ta call it. Ways to try ta keep people safer sos they can do their jobs keepin' other people safe." Ginger pulls a strap on my chest a little tighter and I repress the need to grunt at the surprising force behind it. "Hows about we get our asses in a van and go do just that, huh, doll?"

She swats my ass and saunters ahead of me. The grin that spreads across my face is completely involuntary and I couldn't turn it off if I wanted to.

∗∗∗

The women's barracks are on the east side of the compound. Usually the paths are well lit, keeping it safe for the little ones running around and the elderly when they're coming back from evening activities. Tonight, however, the entirety of the compound is in total darkness aside from the main house which is lit in every manned window. It'll be a matter of who is stealthier and has better equipment at this point, because lights out confirms they knew we were coming.

The Fitzpatrick compound sits at the end of a two mile road up the mountain. Its winding curves are the advantage, most drivers can't make it up without lights, a feat I was impressed Alex tackled. I shouldn't be surprised, given he grew up inside the compound walls and was a supply runner, but I'm impressed, nonetheless.

We wind our way around the west wall in favor of a loading dock with an access into the sewage service entrance, parking all the vehicles in the grove of pear trees several hundred yards back. The hardest part of this whole thing will be the long race back to them if everything goes sideways.

Typically, the loading docks aren't manned, but it seems they're on high alert tonight, because there's five men stationed here at the end of a platform with a single light on over their heads. Alex leads us around a semi still parked in one of only two loading bays, whether to deter us from gaining entrance that way or because they're still loading it, I'm not sure. But they left us an open space without realizing it. We just have to manage to get under the truck in front of the rear wheels without making any noise, climb the stairs silently, and slip down the other side.

Alex goes first, hitting all fours carefully and purposefully moving slowly under the truck. He squats low when he makes it out the other side, waiting. When there's no sort of reaction, he waves Jack and James forward. They're our first line of defense as well as James making up the main muscle in our group. When both men have cleared, Alex waves forward the next bunch and slowly side steps up the stairs, his body creeping low as he goes, his tranquilizer gun at the ready.

I lose sight of him as he makes it to the other side of the platform and turns, slipping off the edge into the tunnel that will lead us to the sewage entrance. Three at a time, all fifteen men make their way under the truck, up the stairs, and over the platform. I watch Ginger duck down low and shimmy herself through. I track her, my eyes never leaving her form. She stands slowly and I quickly follow her. But she's moving too fast and watching the men instead of the stairs. She stumbles on the second one and my hands hit her hips, holding her upright.

Her breath picks up as her lips curl in, worry clear on her face and she stares to her right, waiting for someone to notice. The men continue passing a cigarette around, oblivious to the fact that seventeen people have slipped right behind them.

Ginger scampers across the platform and drops down the other side. I take one last look at the guards, clearly left back here because they're not worried about this being used as an entrance, and follow her into the darkness.

Our pause has put us behind the others, their forms hard to make out even through the infrared goggles with their heat hiding gear on. As we make our way through several turns, the small hints of heat ahead grow larger, however, and our team comes into focus. Jack has already broken off with several others, headed deeper into the compound to help with distractions.

"Plans say we should come up two buildings down from the barracks if we go up right about here," Joe, our map guy says.

"Where does your list say this ladder is?" While I know my way around up top, the turns underground felt like we were going in the wrong direction. I'm unsure if it's because we can't actually see what's around us, or because directions in the dark feel wrong to begin with.

"The system is labeled by meters and cross-points and according to the upper map, we needed to be at twenty two and one fifty-eight." He points over his head at the glowing numbers painted above the ladder. I nod and another man with a dart gun heads up.

The cover makes an awful noise as he moves it aside and then a moment of silence before he knocks his toes on the ladder twice, the signal for all clear. I head up next and turn around to pull Ginger out of the hole. Another two men have cleared the entrance behind us, and we move forward to make space and to get the plan rolling.

The sewers didn't lead us to precisely the right spot as indicated on the maps. Either the maps are old or the configurations for the numbering aren't quite what they believed them to be. We now have to move three buildings down this road, and five buildings up the next one, find a new exit point and hope we don't get lost in the sewers on our way out.

I'm leading the way with Ginger close on my heels when someone behind us coughs. A flashlight flicks on in the distance and a call through my earpiece for "masks down" sounds as I grab Ginger and spin her around the corner of the building we're in front of. Several others make it next to us before the flashlight swings to the corner visible from the street. I pull Ginger's mask down and then seal in my own face.

The masks are lightweight but thick and if I thought it was difficult to see in the dark with the night vision goggles before, I could take that complaint back. Ginger has all but disappeared with her mask down and I realize that the face pieces are also body heat concealing. If it wasn't for the fact that you can't see shit through them, it would be perfect.

We stand perfectly still for several minutes against the cold, concrete wall while the flashlight continues to sweep back and forth across the street making me more and more nervous about how we're going to get children out of here without tails. My hips are pressed into hers and her shallow breathing is loud as hell against my ear. My skin tingles and I itch to run my hands over her despite our precarious situation.

A clear call comes through my earpiece, and I lift my mask. Slowly peeling Ginger's away to reveal wide eyes, her nostrils flaring as she takes too deep of breaths.

"Hey. It's okay. You okay?"

She shakes her head, and I bring my lips to her ear, my words as quiet as I can muster them. "Breathe slower. In for three, hold it, two, three, out through your mouth. Repeat." I breathe with her, afraid to use any more words with someone already suspecting us in this spot.

"We gotta go," James whispers next to me.

"Lead the guys to the next building, we'll be there in thirty seconds."

James nods and motions for the rest of the team to move forward. I watch their backs and when the last one clears our side of the building I turn my attention back to Ginger.

"Nothing is going to happen to you, Red. You have my word."

She nods, still looking slightly panicked but her breathing has leveled out. I raise her head, her stare moving from my chest to my eyes. One hand drifts from the side of her head, my fingertips running a path in front of her ear and across her jaw. I hold her lip hostage with my thumb. It's soft and full and her breath tickles. Unable to resist her I lean forward, hesitating half an inch from her until her hips press forward into mine and I close the space, fusing my lips to her pillowy ones in a soft kiss.

"I've got you. Let's go make this count, okay?" I say as I pull back.

She nods again and her bottom lip tucks under her teeth. Fuck me. I'm a goner but this is not the place or time. Ginger tangles her fingers in mine and we head to the next building, catching up with the rest of the team quickly and working again to the lead. Two more buildings and we'll be there, a standalone at the end of this street. The men's barracks are on the outskirts of the other side of the compound near the main house. It's a strategic set up so there are bodies available in crisis to protect the head honchos. But the women are kept here, in the center of everything, all on its own. It's harder to get to and easily defended from all sides. That's why every plan sucks, but any plan is better than none.

The barracks are dark, save for one tiny light in the middle. My guess would be someone is up with a flashlight or some sort of reading light. Phones wouldn't be allowed in lock down.

The team peels off left and right to check the full parameters of the building and only a few seconds go by before the little robotic voice in my ear sounds a clear signal. I hit my knees in front of the door with my lock kit and get to work. It doesn't take me long to slide the pieces into place and begin a slow turn before I hear a click and the door sags in relief. I look up and down the street both ways before I open the door and Ginger and I slip inside.

As we close the door behind us, several heads turn our way. A soft murmur goes around the room, and I click on the tiny light over my helmet to illuminate my face.

"Dane?" someone croaks out softly.

"You ladies ready to leave?"

Heads whip around to their neighbors and the murmurs get louder.

Ginger takes a step forward, clicking on her light as well. "Shh. The whole place is in lockdown and there's guards everywhere, we gotta move quick and quiet. If ya wanna leave, we have a place for ya. Grab anythin' yous can pack and carry in the next ninety seconds and let's hop."

They look at her intently, gears rolling while they contemplate. Then everyone moves suddenly, like telepathically they all agreed at once. Some of them strip and change clothes quickly, putting extra layers over what they're wearing before shoving clothes and shoes and small belongings into backpacks. Others just pull pants on under their white sleeping gowns and begin stuffing pillowcases with other items. Children watch on in wonder, some looking scared.

I make my way over to Abby, one of the smaller girls, my cousin. She's six and she's never been outside these walls. "Hey, peanut. What's doin'?"

Her eyes meet mine with worry. "Where are we going? Why does mommy look scared?"

"I found you a new place, kiddo, with a room just for you and mommy to share all on your own, and you get your own bed, too. What do you think about that?"

She stares me down for a moment, then her lip quivers. "Why do we have to go in the dark? I don't like the dark."

"Oh sweetie, I know you don't. But there's some people outside that are here to help us, and they could only help us right now. Can you help me, too?"

She nods her head, her face a little less tense. I might not have any kids of my own, but I know one thing; kids love to help.

"Okay, good. It's very important. I need you to help me tell all the kids that we're going to play a quiet game. When we get outside, no one can make a single peep. Everyone who stays quiet can have ice cream with their breakfast tomorrow. Can you do that?"

Abby nods enthusiastically as a smile breaks out on her face. She gives me a quick hug and hops down off her bed to move down the row and tell everyone about our game.

"Oh look, you are a human." Ginger's sudden appearance at my side makes me jump.

"Abby is easy."

"You did good. Look, we got two pregnant ladies. Like very pregnant. It's not gonna be easy gettin' them into the sewer. I think we need ta split the team down and get them goin' now so we don't have so many people standin' around waitin' ta go down. I wanna send them two and the ones without kids. Whatd'ya think?"

It's a risk, not having enough of the team in one group if someone is spotted and the compound goes on alert.

But she has a point. Kids may get anxious staring at the black hole in the ground we're asking them to crawl into and waiting. A single cough put attention on us. What would crying do?

"I think that's smart."

Ginger nods and heads for the door, presumably to tell the others and I turn back to Abby's mom and help her stuff Abby's things into a pack.

"What about her dad?" she asks when the zipper is closed.

"Right now, we're focused on the kids and you all. We'll have to come up with a new plan to get everyone else out that wants to come."

Tears spring to her eyes but she sniffles and nods, wiping them away as quickly as they begin to fall.

"Was everyone moved here tonight? Or are there women in the houses?"

"It's lockdown, Dane. Has been for a few days. Everyone under forty is here."

My attention returns to the door as Ginger, James, and half the team walks through.

"Listen, ladies. This is my friend James. I wouldn't trust nobody else with my life like I do him. He's gonna take some of yous along with his guys ta start movin' everyone out. We don't want too many bodies lingerin' in one place so it's easiest. We gotta be as quiet as we can be. Especially since none of yous are wearing the same kinda gear we are, they can see ya. If you have somethin' dark ta put over yer white gowns, put it on now. If yer pregnant or under twenty-five without a little one, yer headed out now."

Shuffling begins as people hug one another and start making their way to the team. A rapid two knock sounds on the door signaling the all clear and need to move. James starts moving lines of women between guards before urging them to the door. We gather the kids, reminding everyone that silence is the most important part of tonight and they put on brave faces. Everyone stands quietly, waiting for the next one-two knock to signal our turn.

Standing at the edge of the now open doorway, I take a peek down the street. James is taking up the end of the first team and gives our second all clear signal as they disappear around a corner, not even so much as a crunching sound under their boots to signify they were there. Alex is steady beside the door, ready to be our eyes behind us as we make our way back through the dark night. It's eerie how quiet it is. I know there are guards all over, but we're met only with silence as we move past the two buildings before our turn on what is usually an otherwise busy street.

We're halfway to the manhole we came out of when a shrill beep sounds in my ear. James' muffled voice is calling for retreat and shots ring out behind us. Rapid calls of both left and right have me looking to my right where I know Ginger was walking moments ago, carrying Darla's baby because she couldn't carry three children at once. She's frantically looking the other way, trying to spot what might be coming ahead of us where two of Jack's guys are leading us back to the sewers. But the directionals could have been from anyone behind us as well.

Before we make it to the building at the end of the street, a shot whizzes past my head. Ginger ducks and I hit the panic button again, tapping twice in my left ear, where the silent shot came from. The shrill beeping starts again. Jack's voice breaks through the sound yelling "hold" at the same time Damien yells "down" and behind us, mere blocks from where we were, an explosion sounds. The aftermath leaves my ears ringing as the children start crying and the ground beneath my feet rumbles violently.

CHAPTER ELEVEN

Ginger

The baby in my arms is screaming at the chaos as gunfire narrowly misses our team again and again and another explosion booms through the night, this one closer than the last. Jack said our guys were shooting non-lethals. Exploding buildings doesn't seem non-lethal and I send up a silent plea that the buildings are empty, even if some of these men are wicked.

Covering the baby's head with one hand I hold a finger to my earpiece with the other. "James, report."

The line is silent, and my heart begins to hammer in my chest. My demand repeats in my ear, Alex's voice ringing clear and calm through the line. My earbuds make a static sound and fall silent again.

"Damnit, James, report!" I scream into the earpiece. Dane's hand lands on my shoulder, his eyes full of concern as he checks first on me, then over my shoulder. I don't know what he's searching for, but he looks ready to move while I'm rooted in this spot hoping I haven't lost my best friend. "You better not be dead. I'll drag yer ass back from hell by the balls, ya hear me? The devil can get in line after he kisses my ass. James!"

"Reporting," James' voice croaks over the line before he sputters a cough. "We made it to the tunnels, but we got ambushed and weren't able to follow the original route. Joe is trying to figure out which way is up. Don't come down this way, you have to find another way."

He doesn't sound good, but I don't have time to think on it as Dane grunts and pulls me into an alleyway. The women we're moving huddle quickly behind us, many of them have picked up their children and are now trying to calm them while paying attention to what's happening around us with fear clear in their eyes as the gunfire continues in the distance.

This was not the plan. This was not supposed to happen. I look up at Dane whose face is tight in concentration. "Where are we goin', doll?"

"There's an old building in this alley that we haven't used in years because the east wing was crumbling. I haven't been over here in a while but if they didn't do more than just board it up like it used to be, we should be able to walk through the building. It'll run us along the street we were supposed to be on and come out on the backside where they won't be watching for us. I hope."

The pair of men previously in front of us catch up and sweep the sides as Dane leads us further into the complete dark of the alley. Someone behind us sobs and a little voice reassures them.

"Here," Dane states, running his hands over a door frame. "There's no handle but–" He carefully taps his finger along the frame that runs around what looks like a metal door but isn't. Because he's right, there's no handle.

"I need a knife." Alex rushes forward and pulls a blade from his thigh. Dane inspects it momentarily before leaning forward. Light scraping sounds make me nervous. The alley is deathly quiet, despite the chaos at its mouth. Coming out the other end of this building may rely on absolute quiet.

After several painfully anxious minutes, Dane jolts forward, catching the now loose door in the hand opposite of the knife. He blows out a breath, relief heavy on his face, and shifts the door to the side as our point men sweep the space.

A hand comes back out of the mouth of black before us, ushering us forward. Dane pulls me into him for a brief moment, his lips on my forehead before he draws in a full breath through his nose and squeezes my arms. Turning, he laces his fingers through mine and tugs me inside.

It smells damp in here and the sniffles of the little one I'm holding seem to echo slightly through the empty space nearly as loud as the dripping sounds in the corners. I press her tighter to my chest, releasing Dane's hand so I can rub her back, hoping she'll finish calming.

We move quickly through the building, our earpieces calling out left and right directions periodically as we hustle over empty spaces with outlines on the floor like the long room we're in used to hold machinery. Everyone has calmed and moves quietly, clustered close together until finally we come to another door. The light over this door is shining bright, such a stark contrast to all the other lights on our way to the barracks that had been turned out.

Our point men take up either side of the door, their bodies pressed tightly against the wall to look out into the seemingly deserted street. No sound can be heard over the dripping in the corners, they begin communicating exclusively with hand signals. I look up at Dane for an answer to what is happening but he's staring at them just as confused as I am. Then I hear it; a faltered step coming from behind us.

I turn, watching Alex turn just as quickly, training his gun in front of him. He curses, the sound barely audible and fires a shot. A grunting noise precedes a crash to the floor and a loud bang. Alex ducks but the man next to him lets out a noise not unlike a roar before grabbing at his arm. All guns are drawn and multiple shots fire into the darkness as the women huddle together against the far wall and the crying starts again.

Alex turns to us again, his face wide in shock. "Go!"

The men at the door swing it open, sweeping into the street and firing shots as they go. They take several steps and motion us to follow. Dane tucks me behind his back and pushes through the door, his gun at the ready as he moves forward into the night air. My back feels weirdly exposed despite the handful of men still behind me, firing shots at targets I can't see with my goggles on my hairline and no free hands to pull them down.

Several more loud shots break the air before one of Alex's men throws a smoke bomb into the abyss. This close it makes an insane cracking noise and smoke fills the air. Alex and his men turn toward us, running out of the building and closing the door behind them. Alex kicks the handle, bending it toward the frame of the door and begins ushering everyone forward.

Our point men disappear around a left turn just in front of us and we follow, nearly at a running pace now. A door wrenches open to my right and Jack nearly plows me over as he comes out, breathing heavy. His team follows him, sprinting in front of our point men and yelling commands through their earpieces. His team must be on a different frequency, because I don't hear any of them.

We run past several more buildings before coming to a clearing full of tall grass. Beyond that is a perimeter wall. Damien pushes forward through the grass as we all huddle behind Jack and his team. I'm unsure of what is happening until Damien presses what looks like a light colored box onto the wall and sprints back to where we stand.

"Make it quick!" Alex yells from behind us between shots. The men with the lethal bullets are catching up. It almost seems unfair at this moment that ours are meant only to stun when they're shooting to hurt people.

"Heads down!" Damien yells over the noise and everyone squats down into the grass. Jack's team drapes their bodies over several women and smaller children as Dane turns and encompasses me with his height. His back is to the wall and his hands are over the baby's ears as an explosion roars over the sounds of gunfire and screams.

"Up!" The command is loud and clear despite the ringing in my ears. I can't decide if it came through the earpiece, or someone is just that steady among the chaos, but Jack's men begin pulling people from their squatting positions and through the now gaping hole in the wall that's swirling in dust.

Loud bangs and flashes of light go off behind us and I can only hope it's our guys throwing more shit at the men from the compound. They fire wildly through the chaos and a woman close to me screams. Dane curses and pushes me forward toward Jack before sprinting to her side, pulling her up off the ground. He assesses her briefly and encourages her to keep moving. She nods as tears stream down her face and then Jack is tugging me in front of him, pushing at my back and encouraging me to move faster.

The lights of the buses break through the trees as the engines fire up. A few more yards and we'll be in the relative safety of a moving vehicle. The doors on each bus swing open and the point men take up their posts along with Jack's team, covering each one and assisting Alex's team now, firing behind them as they guide women in the right direction and scoop children up, running with them, trying to move faster.

I grab Jack's arm as we approach a bus and pull him to a stop. "James and the ladies?"

"They made it out. Joe took a bullet to the side but everyone else is okay, just banged up. The vans already left." Jack takes the baby from me and pushes me into the open door. "Get everyone in a seat, we have to move. Fast."

I don't hesitate a moment longer on the stairs. The inside of the bus is full of women with uncertain faces, their fear and panic a palpable taste in the air. I move quickly down the rows helping women arrange children safely and make it halfway to the back when Jack rushes up the stairs and barks a command at Damien to get us out of here. A look out the window shows me the rest of the buses are already barreling down the path we used to come in and we're the last ones here.

I take a seat across from Darla as he sets her baby in my arms and runs to the back of the bus, the eyes of the caboose. Damien spins us around, a collective shout sounding at the ferocity of the action that sends everyone careening to the right. The descent down the hill feels like a nightmare, the winding path being taken much too quickly in an effort to put as much distance as possible between us and them so we can make it safely back to the resort without a tail. I knew this was a possibility, and yet, as I hold on with one arm to the seat in front of me, the other wrapped protectively around the innocent child in my arms, tears start flowing at the sheer terror pumping through my veins.

CHAPTER TWELVE

Ginger

The water flowing over me is a welcome distraction. The rivulets running down my face wash away the tracks of the tears I shed just hours ago, when I wasn't so sure our escape was going to work.

Drones, Jack explained. They had drones in the sky. They saw us coming, they saw us sneak in through the docks, disappear into the tunnels, come back up into the streets. They were toying with us.

It was the drones that prompted the initial gunfire we heard as Jack's team shot them from the sky so they couldn't follow us back.

I tip my head up, dunking my forehead into the spray and letting it run through my hair and down my back. The water cascades over my ears as I squeeze my eyes shut. I focus on the rushing sound instead of the echoes of the screams from the ride back here. So many screams.

There's a soft click and I jump, my eyes snapping open.

Dane stands before me, still covered in dirt in all the places his body was exposed as he helped women from the buses and into the main lodge here at the ski resort, their clothes filthy from running through the streets and ducking in the grass as Damien blew up the wall. When I stepped off the bus he was already there, his gear gone, directing people in a simple pair of shorts and a t-shirt. Normal looking, that was the plan. I stripped my own gear to help but when I was ready to fall over, Ellen handed me a cup of tea and directed me to my room to shower and rest. The others went to work patching people up and getting rooms sorted.

"What're ya doin'?" My voice sounds small. Something I so rarely hear.

He doesn't say anything, he just steps forward, pulling my naked body into his own. Dane wraps me in his arms as his chin comes to rest on the top of my head. He takes a shuddering breath. My cheek presses into his chest and I can't help the sob that leaves me. Dane's arms wrap tighter around me, and the flood gates open again, my eyes spilling tears I thought had already dried up. His hands sweep my back and a surprising sway starts.

We stand here like this, the water soothing us both, until my crying stops. "I didn't think we was gonna' make it for a minute there."

"I never would have let that happen." Dane's chest rumbles. I pull away to look up into his face. His eyes look haunted, the frown on his beautiful lips is deep. "I didn't even know we had drones. We couldn't have anticipated it. But I never would have let everyone die."

"I know you wouldn't."

Dane barks out a sharp laugh. "You don't even know me, Red."

"I don't need ta know ya to be able ta see what kinda man ya are, Dane. It really ain't hard ta see ya care."

His eyes search mine, moving left and right between them and his breathing picks up. I can see the turmoil inside him, the fight for control that he's losing as the leftover adrenaline continues to pump through his system and I nod.

Dane's lips come crashing down on mine at the same time his hands dive into the hair on either side of my head. He holds tight, tipping my head back. His hold is demanding as he steps closer, forcing me up onto my toes to meet him and not fall. Raw energy buzzes inside me and I know part of it is the proximity of this man who has been making me crazy for over a week. The other part is that same adrenaline rush we just shared.

Dane's mouth is unyielding, even as one hand drifts to grab my ass and jerk me into his rigid body with a grunt. He lets out a low moan and repeats the motion before his hand drifts lower to my thigh and he pulls my leg up around his hip.

Dane rolls his hips, and I disconnect from our kiss, gasping for air as the warm water trickles down my labia and his wet skin slides over me. In one motion, his mouth attaches to my neck and his other hand grabs my hip, scooping me up like I weigh nothing and pressing me against the glass wall.

He bounces me higher on his stomach, the skin giving a delicious drag as my lips spread and my clit makes direct contact while he latches onto one of my nipples. My fingers bury into his hair on their own and I curl in around him. He flicks my nipple with the tip of his tongue as one hand roams under me seeking my entrance.

When Dane's wandering hand finds what it's been searching for, the rest of him stills. His breath comes out heavy against my ear, his exhale deep and satisfied as he sinks two fingers into me painfully slowly. A sound that can be described only as carnal leaves him and he latches onto my ear with his teeth as he pumps his fingers in me.

My groans fill the space, and it spurs him on, his fingers thrusting harder and his other hand digging into my ass cheek.

"Tell me you don't want my cock buried inside this wet pussy, Red."

I swallow, trying to find my voice. "I can't."

Dane's hold on me slackens as his fingers pull out of me and I slide several inches down his torso. I feel his erection over my clit, the head throbbing as I wiggle against him seeking the friction I need. One hand slams against the wall next to my head as his eyes shutter closed. The other is still holding my ass, rocking me gently against him. A slow pulse begins inside of me, grasping at nothing and demanding more. More of this man who is as intriguing as he is infuriating.

"Tell me you don't want me bareback, babe."

"I can't!" I sob and pull Dane's mouth back to mine. He growls against my lips and rolls his hips again, notching his head and thrusting up into me.

His mouth still fused to mine he swallows the cry that breaks out of me, moaning into my mouth in return. He pulls back and impales me again, slowly. The rigid veins of his cock are pronounced, I can feel them against my walls, dragging over my sweet spot on his way out before the rim of his head follows.

Dane groans, his nose burying itself behind my ear. "You're just as sweet as I dreamed you'd be, Red." His mouth latches on to my neck with another thrust and my pulse rises. "So tight and wet and perfect." Thrust. "So fucking hot." Thrust. "Your pussy is trying to eat me up and I want to let it swallow me whole."

He pulls nearly all the way out and thrusts forward harder, his pelvis slamming into mine. I let out a squeak and it's like a shotgun at the starting line. His thrusts become pistons, firing rapidly to achieve a higher horsepower. I don't make it very long before I feel a climax crash over me all at once.

A deep chuckle leaves Dane, but his pace doesn't slow. Instead, he nips at my lips, teasing them, tasting them before he pushes his tongue against my own, fusing our mouths together once more. He's exploring and driving me wild with his mouth as his hand begins to explore my breast. He pinches and teases my nipple driving me back to the edge, his relentless pace making my head spin.

Dane breaks the hold he has on my lips and drags his tongue up my sternum. He nips my lower lip again and gives my nipple a flick. "Come for me again, babe. Strangle my cock with that sweet pussy of yours."

I shake my head, unable to speak as I crest higher and higher. Not happy with my response, the hand that was on my breast rears back and spanks my ass. The sting shoots straight into my pussy and I jump, crying out.

"I can feel how much you want to come, Ginger. You're so close. Your pussy feels so good. Come on beautiful, let me have it." He bends his knees, his thrusts coming closer together but deeper and harder at this angle.

"No, no, no, no." My chant is punctuated with his short, punishing thrusts as I shake my head. "I can't."

"Yes. Yes, you can. It's mine. Give it to me, Ginger." He growls.

With my name on his lips I break apart, a sob leaving me as my legs clamp around him and my back arches, pushing roughly into the tile behind me. My nipples pull tight, and he leans forward to put one back into his mouth. A shiver rushes down my spine and my hips buck against the added stimulation, my body overwhelmed. He pulls on the nipple, sucking it deeper into his mouth before flicking his tongue rapidly over it. My core clenches around him and I whimper, but he pumps faster and pulls against my nipple again, releasing it and roaring when my body clenches around his once more.

Dane goes almost still, his hips jutting with the spasm of his cock inside me. He sags against me, pinning me between him and the wall as his breathing goes haggard and he rubs his forehead against my chest. I tangle my fingers into his hair and rest my cheek on top of his head. I try to catch my own breath as my walls continue to spasm around him.

"Shit, Red," Dane pants out, his breathing still labored.

"Uh-huh." Is all I can muster.

His arms loosen and he slowly slides me down his body. Feet on the floor, I try to stand but my legs wobble. Dane turns me and pulls me against his body, holding me upright. His arms wrap around me from behind and his hands start a sweep of my body under the water. When his fingers dip into my lips I jolt.

Dane's voice is a whisper in my ear. "You're so sensitive."

My hand cups his as he rubs my lips, dipping in between them every few passes, washing away our combined release.

"Gets that way," I finally reply, incoherently, his sweet ministrations making me breathless.

"How many times can you come, Red?" He kisses the back of my neck before his lips lock over that sensitive space between my shoulder and neck and my head drops back.

Dane's other hand skims over my hip and around the back of me, tucking under my ass and finding my core, two fingers dipping inside and curling. I feel like I'm going to tear into pieces at the intensity of the pleasure he's drawing from my body, pinching my clit on the outside, rubbing my ribbed flesh on the inside. I hear him drop to his knees behind me, my mind registering it only for a moment when he pulls his fingers from me and replaces them with his tongue.

I'm moaning his name as he spears my core and wiggles his stiff tongue inside me, groaning in return like he's devouring the most savory thing he's ever tasted. The hand on my clit ceases its languid rotations and rubs vigorously over me. My legs shake and Dane's hands hit my hips, holding me up while he continues to lap at me mercilessly as I catapult over the edge of another intense orgasm.

When the quivering ceases and I'm dragging in deep breaths, my body so loose I'm barely upright, Dane stands and scoops me up into his arms. He turns and shuts off the water before pushing the door open and grabbing an oversized towel in one hand.

We make our way through the bathroom and then the bedroom. He sets me on my feet and tucks me into his side long enough to pull back the covers on the bed and spread out the towel. Placing me on the towel, he retreats to the bathroom and comes out less than a minute later, looking hastily dried and with another towel in his hands.

Dane crawls in next to me and dries my back before squeezing my hair and gently rubbing the towel over my arms and hips. He throws it to the side of the bed and covers us both up, pulling me into his chest.

I sigh against him, and he kisses the top of my head. "That good, huh?"

"Don't flatter yerself." I push against his shoulder, and he chuckles. But my grin spread over his chest gives me away and I wonder how the hell I ended up in this bed completely speechless.

CHAPTER THIRTEEN

Dane

Ginger is sound asleep as the sun starts creeping through the break in the curtain. Her creamy skin is such a contrast against my bronzed tone. Everything about her looks delicate and porcelain including her flawless complexion, interrupted only by spreads of freckles across her nose and chest. I feel pride in getting to see them, if only because I took a plunge and interrupted her shower so the face I'm looking at this morning is completely free of make-up.

There's light noises and the low murmur of voices coming from down the hall that leads to the kitchen. Carefully, I work to disentangle her limbs from my own. She sucks a deep breath in through her nose and her back arches, stretching as she rolls. After a few moments, I decide she isn't going to wake up so I roll out of my side and begin hunting for clean clothes. These rooms are supposed to be stocked with plenty of sizes for all the guys.

I manage to find boxer briefs, jeans and a polo shirt, all in black, *go figure*. Dressed, I look at Ginger again, peacefully curled around a pillow with that wild orange hair splayed across the bed. I lean down and land a kiss on her shoulder, promising myself I'll be back before she wakes up. In the kitchen, I find Jack, Alex and James pouring over yet another map. "How'd the night go?"

All three men look at me at the same time. Alex purses his lips in annoyance but it's James that speaks up. "We took Joe to the hospital a few towns over. He just got out of surgery. He's going to be fine, but he's mighty pissed. We left a guy with him just in case. Ara–"

"Why didn't you tell us there were drones?" Alex snaps before James can tell me how Araia is doing with the bullet that grazed her shoulder.

"I've never seen a drone anywhere in the compound. Ever."

"I don't believe you." The distaste and distrust are bleeding over his features. Normally stoic Alex lost his poker face and I'm looking at the rage that's left behind. "Do you know how many people we almost lost last night? Kids, Dane!"

"I didn't know! I'm the one who asked you all to go in to get them out. Do you think I'd have done that if I thought there would be fucking drones on us?"

Alex takes several paces forward, his toes nearly touching my own. "How do we know it wasn't a ploy to get us all back in there to begin with?"

"What purpose would that serve? It's not like he can force any of you to do anything." I get where he's coming from. They didn't have any reason to trust me going into this.

Jack steps up behind Alex, putting a hand firmly on his shoulder. "Come on, brother. We have things to figure out and we could use another set of eyes. You know as well as anyone that no one in that place knows everything. It's better to keep people dumb." His eyes meet mine and I narrow my own but let it go as he turns his back and steps to the head of the map again.

"What are you looking at?" I ask and Jack waves me over.

"The layout of the apartment building. It's secure enough, but there aren't enough emergency exits, especially for the upstairs. It's up to code, but if something happens and they need to vacate quickly, it won't be for a fire where the hallways serve their purposes, it'll be because people are sweeping the building. We're trying to work out which apartments to connect, and how we can put up exits on the second through fifth floors that can't be used against them."

I look over the blueprints, my mind putting me back in the building room for room. There were only three apartments on either side of the main hallway and two across from one another on the other side of the elevators. Eight apartments in total per floor. While elevators are a quicker escape than stairs that men would most certainly be on, they could be staked out on the main floor. Unless–

"Is there room for a rear entrance and exit on the elevators?"

"Like a carded system like they use in hospitals?" James tilts his head.

"Exactly like that." I sweep my hand across the three apartments that are on the same wall as the elevator. "These apartments. We could connect the two on the left with an elevator access card and build a hallway between the two that share a wall with the elevator. A rear entrance you can only use with a key card. Drop it into the basement and make that emergency access only with another keycard that only allows exit. That would give fifteen apartments a locked up escape. Give the connecting apartments to families who wouldn't mind the person next door having access to their apartment. Sisters, cousins, things like that."

Jack has been pensive looking; he rubs his chin and nods. "That's some good thinking, kid. Now what about the other twenty five apartments?"

By the time we work out escape routes, including one panic room on each floor for the one isolated apartment that we all agree isn't the best plan but is a needed option, and remote operated drop-down ladders into ventilation that we'll increase the height on, it's nearly noon and everyone's stomachs are growling. Miriam and Ellen are already bustling around the stoves working on various meals to help the kitchens in the main lodge feed the small army we brought in late last night, so I return to my room.

The door is closed like I left it, but I hear muffled music coming from inside. My curiosity gets the better of me and I turn the handle, careful to not make any noise. Peeking my head in, I spot Ginger in front of the dressers. Her hair is wet and she's wearing nothing but black cheeky underwear.

Her hips swing to the right as she dips down, repeating the action to the left. Shooting upright she slowly bends forward, her hands dragging down the front of the dresser as she lifts her heels alternately, the rounds of her ass cheeks bouncing and catching my attention.

My arms are crossed over my chest and my head is turned, assessing every delicious inch of her backside when she turns and sees me. She jumps and lets out a shriek then claps her hands over her mouth.

"Oh my god ya perv! How long were ya standin' there?"

I don't answer her, I just adjust my jeans instead. Her eyes track my movement, and I cock an eyebrow before I head to the armchair in the corner of the bedroom.

I claim my spot and motion for her to come this way. She crosses her arms over her shapely breasts and pops a hip. She's shooting daggers at me, but I'm not even phased by them. This woman is an absolute hellcat, and I happen to like a little wild, I'm not afraid of the fight.

"Who the hell taught ya yer manners?" she snaps at me.

"Oh, Red, there's nothing polite about what I intend to do to you. No manners needed." I feel the shit eating grin spread across my face as I envision exactly where I want her dancing, and it isn't across the room, and I don't intend to be able to watch it.

"Respect yer elders!"

"I–what?"

"I am older than you, bub. Ya got the one up on me last night because I was stuck in my feels, doll. But yer not in charge and I don't listen to demands, ya hear me?"

Thoroughly confused that she's pointing out her age and literally scolding me, I bark out a laugh. I can't help it; it rolls through me, chasing out the tension that's been building back up through the back and forth this morning over escape plans and shit I don't want to have to consider. I lean back in the chair, steepling fingers over my forehead while I try to catch my breath and control the laughter.

"Glad I'm amusin' ya." Ginger waves me off and stomps back to the dresser she was grinding on earlier. She yanks open a drawer and pulls something out at random, throwing the black t-shirt over her head and making for the bathroom.

Oh no, she's not getting away that easy. I jump up out of my seat and make it across the room before she crosses the threshold, grabbing her hips and dragging her backward. She lunges forward, her feet scrambling, trying to make purchase where they're dangling a few inches over the wooden floor. When I reach the bed, I turn her, scooping her up again and bouncing her on the bed. Her eyes widen and she scrambles back several feet just to be caught instead by an ankle.

I wasn't kidding when I told her she didn't know me. She's poking a bear with the stubborn defiance she clearly wields as her usual weapon of choice. We'll war it out then and see who is still standing at the end.

"You're going to hear me, Red. That little booty dance gave me a very specific vision. I'm a patient man, but I like to see all my dreams come true and I don't stop until I've got every single fucking detail right." Grabbing the end of the t-shirt, I give it a sharp tug at the seam on the side.

The material splits open while Ginger's eyes go wide, and I keep tugging while I finish making my point. "This offensive t-shirt was not in the vision I had of you finishing your dance to that dirty, dirty song on my face, Red."

Ginger swats at me when I get more than halfway up the shirt and her ribs are exposed. I climb up the bed and pin her hips down between my knees and tug harder, slitting the seam around the arm and all the way to the neckline.

"Get the hell off me, Dane! Ya arrogant little prick." She's struggling and my dick is getting stiff behind this damn zipper.

I use both my hands to pull the neckline. It takes a bit of grunt, but it too tears apart, leaving her gorgeous tits exposed. Free and taught, her nipples call to me as her chest heaves from her struggles. I pinch them both and then scoop her breasts up in my hands. She groans and stops fighting me, her nails digging into the backs of my arms as she vice grips my biceps.

"If you actually want me to stop, this is when you say so." Ginger shakes her head and bites into her lower lip as she tries to grind her hips into me.

I slide down her body and grind my jean clad cock against her. She groans and my name leaves her on a soft breath. The cherry red of her lips is inviting, and I dip into her for a gentle kiss. Her tongue runs over my lips and it's my turn to echo a groan back to her as my dick jumps. I open for her, giving her this bit and she lunges into it with a ravenous demand that surprises me.

Ginger nips at my lips in between sweeps of her tongue and needy whimpers. She tugs me into her by my shoulders, her nails a welcome bite of pain weaving into the ecstasy of our grinding. I run my hands down her sides, feeling every goosebump adorning her skin and grip her hips. My control is fracturing with the way she's meeting my grind and clinging to me. My fingers dig in, determined to hold her still until she breaks the kiss and drops her head back, her torso arching off the bed.

Wrapping my arms under her, I scoot the few feet off the bed and stumble back to the chair. Ginger sheds the destroyed t-shirt as my ass hits the edge of the seat and I push her up to my shoulders. The chair wraps nicely behind my shoulders, practically a cocoon around us with high arms that aren't really usable except that they're a fantastic height for Ginger's feet.

She looks at me skeptically, but I answer her with a growl. She looks like she wants to say something, and I don't want to hear it. Grabbing her chin, I press my thumb in her mouth, holding her captive.

"Miriam is cooking in the kitchen, but I want my dessert first today. Be a good girl and feed me, Red."

Her tongue twirls around my thumb and I'm beginning to regret the decision to do this in this chair. But now I'm committed, so I push her up again and she goes less reluctantly, placing her thighs at the edge of my shoulders and her feet on the arm rests while I support her with a cheek in each hand.

I run my nose up the soaked panties in front of me and she jumps before she groans deep in her throat. This woman makes something inside me feel primal, and every time she gives me a noise, I lose a little more of the barrier holding it all in. Estimating, I give a gentle bite over her clit and am rewarded when her legs clench me, and she hisses air in. One of her hands moves from the high back of the chair to my head, her fingers tangling in my hair. Ginger is so sensitive, and it feeds my ego, not that it needs it.

Shoving her panties to the side I go for her clit again, sucking it in sharply then pulsing around it. She bounces on her feet and a smile spreads on my face. I want to know everything that makes this woman tick, if only so I can use it against her again and again.

"Dance," I demand and point my tongue for a slow dance of my own. The positioning is difficult, but she moves her hips in a stirring motion, rolling herself into my face and I groan my approval.

I keep pace with her, swirling the tip of my tongue around her clit again and again. The pace is slow and she's shivering as she mounts higher. I can feel her pussy pulsing, grabbing, searching. I want to fill it up, but I want to finish this dance first.

Just when it feels like she's about to come and my adrenaline spikes in anticipation, she scrambles off me abruptly enough that I don't have a chance to reach out and keep her in place. Ginger drops to her knees in front of me and makes quick work of the button and zipper on my jeans.

I raise my eyebrows in surprise, and she locks eyes with me as she slowly sinks her mouth over my head. Her cheeks suck in and she rolls her tongue around the rim. My head drops back, and I groan, sinking my fingers in her hair. Ginger swats my hands away, pulling her mouth off me.

I start to protest but she gives me a glare. "Hands to yerself."

I put my hands up in surrender and grin. I'll play whatever game she wants as long as she puts her mouth on me again.

"Good boy," Ginger purrs before sliding slowly down my shaft. She bobs a few times, taking me at a languid pace until I thrust deeper into her mouth impatiently.

She makes a noise that's clearly a scold and freezes her movements as her eyes snap up to mine. Message received. Suctioning back on my head, she runs her tongue through my slit and my eyes roll back. Her hot mouth is heaven enough, but then she adds torture to the lineup. I roll my lips in to avoid the biting demand on the tip of my tongue. I'm desperate to take over, but I don't want her to stop again.

Ginger stands a little taller on her knees and braces her forearms on my thighs as she slides every last centimeter of my shaft into her mouth. She sucks a deep breath in through her nose when I let out a curse and then relaxes her throat and pushes me in a little deeper. Her lips are pressed into my skin and my head is hitting the soft flesh of her throat. Then she swallows.

"Jesus fuck, Red!" My hips jolt from the vice grip it causes, and she gags as she slaps a hand on my leg. My apology is cut short when she swallows again, then again and I pant, my hands flying to grip the back of the chair. I blow out a heavy breath and my next groan comes out in a strangle caught in my throat.

The sight of her impaled on my cock, tears spilling from her eyes, hair wild around her face, stirs the heat in me. The control it's taking not to grab her head and fuck her face while I enjoy the sight only adds fuel to that flame.

"I'm gonna come, Ginger." My thighs shake slightly from the effort of keeping my pelvis still so she can assault my cock, and I feel it spasm in her mouth. She gives me a wicked grin I feel in my balls.

And then she pulls off.

"Not yet yer not." Ginger stands and turns, grabbing the sides of her panties and dragging them slowly down her legs while she bends over.

Her hands are at her ankles, one foot delicately lifted like she's going to remove the underwear as slowly as she sunk her mouth down my shaft and my resolution vacates.

Lunging into her space I slap both hands on her ass and grab hold. She yelps and tries to turn but the motion makes her wobble with my hold on her and the black panties still around her ankles, so she stays where she is. "Are you playing with me after you just denied me, Red? That's a dangerous fucking game."

"Bossy, demanding, and threatening. You're somethin' aren't ya? What're ya gonna do, Dane? Bend me over yer knee and spank me? Tie me down and make me beg? My word is freckle, ya wanna make me scream it?"

Her words are like speed soaring through my system. I revel in the feel of it, my body wanting more. More of her, more of the thrill, more of the fuel it gives me. My blood is rushing in my ears with each new question her sultry tone spits out. She's so turned on I can see the arousal in the afternoon light coming through the window next to us.

"Hellcat." The word leaves me like a curse as I pull her into my lap, right over my waiting cock. I slam her down in one thrust and our groans leave us together.

Ginger kicks the underwear off her ankles and I spread her thighs wide over my own. I lean back, pulling her knees up over my elbows as her back hits my chest. She hiccups a breath into her lungs as my head resettles inside her, sliding over that amazing, ribbed flesh that sparks the nerves over my own sensitive underhead. She was already tight, but her legs pulled apart like this, stretched as far as they'll go, she's impossibly tighter, her pussy squeezing me. I won't last like this but it's not going to stop me.

I jerk my hips, and she moans, the sound music to my ears. Every sound, every inhale, they're mine and it's intoxicating. When she wraps her hands around my neck and grabs onto my hair I lose it; that last tendril of control. I widen my stance, pushing her wider by a fraction and get the leverage I need to let loose. My pace is feverish, and her cries are incoherent. When she comes the first time, her back tries to arch off of me but the position makes it impossible and all she manages is to push herself down harder as I curl my body around hers, my head over her shoulder.

"Do you see what you do to me, Red? Do you see what happens when you play games and work me up? When you fuck around?" I thrust hard and she whimpers, her thrashing head landing the sound right in my ear.

"I like to rile ya up," she whispers, her voice shaky. "Oh fuck, I like it so much."

A growl rips out of me when she turns her head and fuses her lips to mine, her tongue pushing into my mouth. I swallow down the keening sound she feeds me as her pussy strangles my cock again. I soar off the edge of my own orgasm with her.

Her legs start quivering and she breaks the kiss to lean forward when I let them go and run my hands over her stomach, drawing her against my chest, my face pressed into her back. We're both panting and shaking and I know in that moment, I'm completely fucked. Because there's no way I'm ever going to get enough of her.

"Lunch!" Ellen's voice calls pleasantly through the door as she plants a light knock on it and giggles. Ginger follows suit, giggling as she lays draped over me.

"Now I need another shower."

CHAPTER FOURTEEN

Ginger

"That doesn't solve the problem with medical records, identification, transcripts. How are they supposed to get jobs or go to the doctors, or even get a car for that matter?" Ellen has been asking questions throughout lunch and is back to ranting at Jack as they wash dishes, and I dry them. We talked to some of the teenagers this morning and the morale is low as we try to navigate through the areas we hadn't considered prior.

"I really haven't figured that part out yet, kitten. It was the getting them out part I was worried about. As long as they know their socials, we can get them new documents." His point is valid, but he's missing the most important part.

"What about them kids?" I ask, pointing out the elephant in the room.

Jack sighs, "Most of them probably don't even have social security numbers. I think we should sort out the adults first, and work on figuring out who needs what. Break them down into groups and go through everything with each one of them."

"You really think interrogatin' a bunch of scared women is gonna get ya anywhere?"

"I wasn't suggesting we interrogate them. But Ellen isn't wrong, we need information. We need to know what they need to move beyond the next few months. Especially because we have more than a few pregnant women."

"What do you think, Ginger?" Ellen dries her hands on the towel hanging in front of her and looks at me.

"I think you should call those girlfriends of yers and get 'em up here. We sure ain't sendin' any of these brutes in to chat with the rest of the ladies. They're shaken enough."

A plethora of expressions cross Jack's normally stoic face. He grabs another dish out of the rinse water and shakes it off, taking the towel from me and drying it himself. "Okay then. Ellen will make the calls. We'll leave a team here to keep the perimeter secure, and I'll take the rest of the guys back into the city to help with the repairs, speed things up. You'll call me if shit goes south. Clear?"

My eyebrows raise at his tone, but his face remains a firm demand of what he wants. I consider arguing for a moment, but his jaw ticks, the thought of defiance setting him on edge in a way I've never seen in the many years we've spent together.

"Alright, boss man. You got it."

"Jesus, that's wrong coming out of your mouth. I need everyone safe, that's it. You're in charge." He swipes his palm down his face and turns to kiss Ellen and rub his hand over the baby before he leaves.

He's out of the room for no more than three seconds before Ellen loses hold of the laugh she was hiding, and we both break into hysterics.

Late into the evening, Kiley arrives with Jenny and Jenny's cousin Ember. I've never met Ember, but Jenny talks about her quite a bit. We pow-wow over tea and decide to let the women rest tonight, going over groupings and the best way to approach. Ellen pulls out our list of names and is getting ready to pass it around when Kiley snatches it from over her shoulder.

"What the fuck?" Her eyes widen. "Not possible."

Ellen turns, looking at her quizzically.

"Jayla Thomas is my cousin," she says.

"She's on the list?" Jenny asks the same question that was on my own tongue.

"She shouldn't be. My aunt got involved with one of the guys in that god forsaken place. He was mean though, like real mean, and controlling. She said she sent Jayla out to California with her dad to get her away from there. I haven't seen her in years. Where's Jayla? Why–"

Jenny steps forward and wraps Kiley in a hug, cutting off her panicked rapid-fire questioning.

Ellen's head tilts as she assesses the pair of them. "This is why you're always digging at Jack, isn't it?"

"Where's Jayla?" Kiley asks again.

Ellen pulls the list from her hands and tracks down it as I move closer to look for myself. "She's only seventeen? She's with the kids. Wanna go get her?"

Tears well in Kiley's eyes and she rushes for the door. Ellen looks at me skeptically, but I give my head a subtle shake and meet Kiley at the door, ready to head to the main lodge and find Jayla.

When we're outside, Kiley tips her head to the sky and draws a deep, shaky breath into her lungs. It comes out on a sob, and I wrap my arms around her.

"My aunt never made it out," she confesses. "They told us she got sick and refused treatment and that the cancer was too far advanced and took her quickly, but we knew. Anytime we did see her she was either caked in make-up or covered in bruises. He killed her."

"It's over now, doll," I whisper against her shoulder and rub her head while she cries. "We got yer cousin out, and all the girls she grew up with. We made it and a few folks got hurt, but everyone's gonna be okay. It's gonna be okay."

We stand there a few minutes until Kiley shudders in another breath and sighs then stands up straight and wipes her eyes. "Let's go."

The remainder of the walk to the lodge hangs with heavy silence. The women inside that lodge have been through so much. I understand the grief that accompanies the relief when you're safe. It's wrapped in fear and doubt and is like a brick in your chest. The somber silence earlier today was hard to wade through as we started talking to the younger ones, trying to find out if they knew of any family they had outside the compound, and that silence hangs around me now.

I interviewed Jayla. She didn't have any answers about family. She didn't know of any other than her mother who was gone. If Kiley hadn't seen her in years, there would have been a great enough number of them to have erased the thought from Jayla's head.

Idle chatter greets us at the threshold when we step into the blast of warmth that's so very different from the brisk evening weather at our backs. Several faces look up from what they're concentrating on when we pause in the doorway. Women are gathered at a round table near the entrance of the large sitting space with steaming mugs in front of them. Children are at another table scattered with crayons and papers as a few adults sit at the head of it deep in conversation. My eyes scan the room looking for the young woman I spoke to not more than a few hours ago; Jayla. She's in an oversized armchair adjacent to the fireplace in the center of the big room, curled up with a book. Kiley's eyes land on her shortly after my own and she's across the room before I can warn her that she may not remember her, scooping the younger girl into her arms. They're both crying when I turn away and I know it'll be okay.

My job is over, I cannot bring myself to follow Kiley. This is her moment, her peace. She's lived with this sadness for so long and she doesn't need an audience for the tears of relief she's sharing.

CHAPTER FIFTEEN

Dane

The apartments are a mess. Phil's men have been working around the clock in two teams, Phil himself never leaving the site. He's camped out front in what looks like a panic room on a trailer, which would be hilarious if it wasn't a fairly accurate depiction of necessity with the people we're dealing with. Even with all those men there all day and night, only the first two levels are done, and we've run into a massive problem; someone stripped the electrical right out of the walls. Pulled it out through the connection in the basement.

When Phil relayed the news and what his electrician said it was going to cost, not to mention the three extra days it was going to take to run, Jack turned and shot me a look of utter irritation before telling Phil to bring in a second team and get it done in two and storming out of the building. I may have given the man a hassle about living high in an ivory tower, but the last few days have shown me that Jack is anything but a greedy king on a throne.

We spend the rest of the day helping the crew clean out the trash, the dumpster has been hauled away twice and replaced by fresh ones. How they managed to decimate this building in such a short amount of time is astonishing. It's nearing dawn hours when I nearly bump into Ginger as I'm coming around the side of the dumpster headed back to the building.

"What are you doing here? It's late."

Ginger raises an eyebrow at my questioning. "Nice ta see ya, too. Didn't know ya were my keepa."

I lift a hand to my face, ready to swipe it down when I remember the state of my hands and think otherwise. "I didn't mean it like that, shit, it's late, I'm tired."

Her voice is soft when it sounds again. "I came ta getcha after I talked ta Jack inside. He's ready ta wrap the teams up fer the night. Most the guys are goin' home instead of back to the resort since we're already here. Thought ya might like a ride home with me?"

There's an air of confidence surrounding her and her body is turned into mine. It's not just a suggestion veiled in her offer of a ride, it's a knowing declaration of her intention.

"I like when a woman knows what she wants."

"What do I want, doll?"

I yank her hips flush with my own and grind into her, leaning into her ear and dropping my voice. "Why don't you finally show me that room you disappear into, and I'll show you?"

"My room? Ya wanna tarnish my space, Fitzpatrick?" She grins up at me. Her eyes are heavy with mischief, and I let the name slide as I realize she's trying to get a rise out of me.

I purse my lips, mocking thought. "I suppose my bed is big enough for two people if they don't mind a tight space. Damien might not appreciate the show. But then again, I don't know him well."

A laugh bubbles out of Ginger, and she scoffs as she comes up on her tiptoes and places a chaste kiss on my lips. I grin in return when she saunters away and calls me to follow with a crook of her finger over her shoulder.

✳✳✳

When we park on the street at Ginger's, I take stock, remembering the last time we were here. The lights have been fixed and the street looks calm, all the doors closed up tight. I head to the door leading upstairs, fishing for my keys, but Ginger touches my elbow and smiles softly at me, motioning to the business door next to us.

Silently, she pulls her keys from her purse and opens the door, flicking on the familiar red light and locking the door behind us. She leads me through a doorway bathed in darkness and I take in the vintage looking hallway beyond it, with its old school carpets and mysterious series of doors. We pass several before she stops at one on the left marked 'private' and inserts her keys in the lock again.

"What's this?" I ask, motioning to a red button next to the door.

"Panic button."

My eyebrows draw in and she lets out a laugh. "Trouble is, doll, no one's here ta come runnin' if ya push it tonight," she says with a wink.

She opens the door and ushers me inside, flipping on a light. The room is a mix of black, white, and grey. A large bed is set in the center with its grey, block headboard creeping up the wall and a frame of lights outlining the wall and illuminating the space before the bed. The lights reflect on a polished marble floor, broken up only by the soft runner rugs on either side of the bed. The only personal looking touch in this room are the floor to ceiling black bookcases full of books and covered in small trinkets.

I make my way to the shelves, perusing the titles that look to be mostly classic literature with a mix of modern mystery titles. I pick up a small box and flip the lid. Music plays and a ruby red stone twirls over a mirror.

"They're all gifts from women whose lives we've touched here," Ginger says, her hands running up my back under my shirt.

"And how do you do that?"

"We make 'em feel whole. It takes love, and trust. Friendship. Understanding. And they learn. First, they learn how ta say no. Somethin' these kinda women weren't taught by their parents. Good little society girls sit quiet, and listen, we train that outta them. Then they learn ta expect all those good things from the people they let into their lives, but also from themselves. How ta not accept less than what they deserve. And it makes 'em feel seen again as somethin' other than a prize on someone's arm or just a body in their bed."

"Where does that leave you?"

"How so?" she asks, a look of confusion clouding her expression.

"Who sees you, Ginger? You have all these men working for you to better the lives of women you don't even know until they find you. Who helps you? Where's your happily ever after?"

I could hear a pin drop from across the room and its subsequent roll across the floor with the way Ginger has frozen in front of me. She stares into my eyes with a sadness so profound bleeding through hers that it makes me want to rip my heart out of my chest and present it to her.

"I missed it." She swallows and blinks her eyes slowly. "I never wanted ta be a mom, never wanted ta rely on no man, never wanted ta be stuck in the cycle my own mom couldn't get outta. Or wouldn't, I dunno sometimes. So, I didn't go lookin' for it. I didn't want it, see? Don't look here for no happily ever after, Dane. I can't give ya that."

I nod, not with agreement to what she's saying, but understanding and acknowledgement that this isn't a subject we're going to be able to work through tonight, on little sleep and after such a heavy day. "And what about the bed?" I ask, nodding in that direction in an effort to change the subject to something less heavy.

"Well, love, this one is my personal room. It gets loud upstairs and sometimes a girl just wants some peaceful beauty rest, ya know? Now, go take a shower. Ya smell." She slaps a towel and a pair of sweats on my abs and points across the room to another closed door. "I'll be right back."

I watch her walk out the door we came in and look down at the fabric in my hands. I surrender myself to the silence of the unfamiliar room and the knowledge that the sun is coming up outside in just a few hours then make my way to the bathroom.

My shower is anything but silent though, my mind running through the events of the last few days and all the ways I could have handled things differently to come to a less daunting result. Regardless of how things have come to fruition, I cannot change what has already been but as I sit down on the bed and work the towel over my hair, I wonder if maybe I can work with Ginger to help the women we got out move through the trauma that has surrounded their lives, to help them the way she has helped so many women seeking a different outlook on love. We got them out to make things better for them, to give them a real future, after all.

The bed behind me dips just slightly, bringing me out of my thoughts. A smile graces my lips, ready to use them on her and I begin to turn before a wisp of something cool slides over my eyes.

Ginger's lips are at my ear as she secures the fabric behind my head, her voice low and sweet. "Sit still, lover."

"What's your game, Red?" I clear my throat, my voice feeling thick and stuck in it when she scratches her fingertips over the base of my skull and travels down my neck. My dick jumps in my sweats when she rakes them across my chest and leans her bare breasts against my back. She nips at my ear and then her weight disappears from the bed.

The room buzzes with silence aside from her delicate step on the rug. I stand and take a tentative step into the space in front of me, knowing it's an empty space. My head tilts, waiting for a sound that never comes. I take another step into the abyss and her fingertips graze lightly over my abs. I grab into the air but miss her.

"I could love every inch of you without my eyes, Ginger. When I find you–" her airy laugh interrupts my threats, and I gravitate to the sound.

I reach a hand out, tentative. I don't find her, but her hand drags lightly across my shoulders, her hair skimming my spine as she passes behind me. A shiver follows her touch, and I inhale a deep breath as I feel my cock swell. Turning into the space she just occupied, I catch her lingering scent. I inhale a little deeper, eating up the creamy coconut from her lotion and the way it mixes deliciously with the mint and lime of her conditioner. But under it all is her, the sweet musk of her arousal that has me groaning as I follow the scent like a hound.

I can feel her around me, my body buzzing in anticipation. Ginger waits, taunting me, and I relax my body to hone in on my senses. Willing the rushing sound of my heart in my ears to quiet, I tilt my head up and listen, catching her slightly shaky breathing. She's as excited as I am.

No sooner do I turn into the sound than it disappears. Ginger's fingers touch my waist tentatively and her lips graze up my spine before she bites softly into my shoulder. I take too long enjoying the sensations and she's gone. I huff a laugh and follow the scent again, pressing forward to the door then turning so my back is facing the wall. Two can play dirty.

I wait, searching with my hands and listening for movement. Ginger is quick and quiet. I barely notice the shift beside me before she's running another piece of silky fabric up one of my arms and across my shoulders. Not willing to play this game all morning, I take the last few steps backward and pin her to the door.

"Usin' yer height advantage? No fair," she whispers.

I turn, her naked body pressing into my chest. My skin feels like it's vibrating and her skin on mine only amplifies it. She jumps into my arms as I scoop her up around her ass and stomp back to the bed. I have to orient myself at the side to make sure I won't throw her off the end as I deposit her roughly against it and climb over her legs. True to my words, I leave the blindfold on and take her lips. I was serious when I said I didn't need my eyes, because every inch of my body knows every inch of hers.

She moans into my mouth when I squeeze her tit in one hand, the other fisted in her hair. I take that moan, greedy for more. There's a frenzy building inside my body born from the fire she lit with her teasing, and I stoke it with her taste, plunging my tongue into her mouth over and over until she's panting and wriggling under me.

Tearing my mouth from hers, I take a second to catch my breath and crawl down her body, latching onto one nipple and then the other before making my way to my actual destination. Ginger opens her legs for me, and I nip my way up a thigh as I press her legs wider to lay her knees open, knowing her pussy is on full display and ready for me.

I drag my lips the rest of the way across her, grinning when I find her labia and pull it between my teeth. She hisses at the contact and swats at my head. My chuckle answers her before I nip the other lip the same way and she squirms, her knees pulling up.

"You stay where I put you," I scold her, pressing her knees back down.

Ginger grabs my head and presses down. "Then you stay there and do yer job," she jabs back at me.

"You started this tease, Red."

"Shut up and eat me, Dane."

This is what does it for me with her. This power play, her demands, the fearlessness with which she gives them despite my clear intention to rule her body. And I'm powerless to deny her. So, I do exactly what she tells me to and dive into her, my tongue spearing inside as my lips make contact. She cries out and grabs my hair as her hips buck at the quick invasion. Her cry turns to a moan as I plunge a few more times, lapping at the sweetness I love so much before I draw my tongue out and replace it with two fingers so I can find her clit.

Ginger continues to tug at my head, her hips moving in time with my strokes in and out while I flick and twirl my tongue around her clit, lapping, nipping. She grips my fingers and her hips stutter in their timing, and I know she's close.

I draw her swollen little bud between my teeth and reach a hand up, toying with a nipple while I search with my other hand for the ribbed flesh inside her. She groans and shivers when I've zeroed in on it and I shake my fingers over it, rubbing vigorously and smiling in victory as her moans get louder and her back arches off the bed. My dick is weeping inside my pants, and I couldn't care less because making Ginger come is euphoric. I could do this all night long every night, letting the sun come up before I nut, and it would be perfection.

Ginger lets out a little shriek and her hips buck uncontrollably as her pussy pulses around my fingers, riding the wave of her climax. I pull my fingers out when she relaxes and give her pussy a little smack that makes her groan then crawl over to the other side of the bed, dropping my pants as I come to my feet. I reach blindly for her, finding her shoulders and tugging her to the edge.

Ginger gives a little squeak when I have her shoulders at the edge, and she grabs my thighs. The thrill of still not being able to see her as I grab her face and slide my fingers into her mouth is starting to make me feel absolutely feral, and I give my cock a few pumps. When she's moaning around my fingers, I pull them out, using the saliva she's left behind to pump a few more times then slide my cock between her lips.

This angle feels glorious, my dick sliding perfectly along her tongue and fitting into the little dip in the back. She has very little control here and I give it a little pump to seat myself deeper. She inhales through her nose and grips my thighs, moaning around my dick when I pull out of her throat.

"Fuck yeah, baby, swallow my dick."

Leaning forward, I push myself into her again and reach in search of her pussy. She's sprawled on the bed, her head over the edge, making it easy to touch her. I only wish I could see how hot this scene must be. Deciding I'll repeat this particular moment again, I press my fingers back into her. Ginger shivers and her mouth tightens around me. My fingers pump into her furiously as my hips do the same and

I'm lost to sensation, swimming in the high of her greedy mouth devouring me as her pussy tries to pull my fingers in further in the same way.

My cock pulses and brings me back to the very real knowledge I'm too close to coming. And while I love coming down Ginger's throat, I'm not done with her yet.

I pull out of Ginger's mouth, and she protests with a whimper. She starts to say something in that sassy tone, but I lean over her, cutting off whatever it was when I clasp my mouth back over her clit, not relenting until she's shaking with release again.

I don't let her catch her breath this time as I crawl onto the bed, hooking one of her ankles over my shoulder and secure my knees. Ginger wraps her other leg under my ass as I tug her to me and slam home in the same movement, one stroke seating me tight against her. The sound Ginger makes is guttural and strangled and I moan in response. Her breath heaves in and out while her walls still pulse around me. No way am I going to make it through this.

"Feel that, Red? This pussy is mine. Feel how much she loves me? How she begs for it?" I thrust slowly into her, dragging out all the sensation trying to slow my body's need to dominate her and wind her higher at the same time.

She mews when I sink back in and hold myself there a moment before giving her a few quick jabs deeper, despite our flesh being tight against each other. I drag myself all the way out, notching my head to her entrance and pausing before I thrust sharply back in. She lets out a sob as her legs start to shake. I revel in the way she allows herself to be powerless against me the same way I lose my own power when she speaks. The way her trust is so freely handed to me every time she opens her body and allows me inside it. Trust I never would have thought I could earn in this lifetime with the ugliness I was born from and the unlovable parts of me I've spent years trying to hide. But this woman, this woman sees every piece of it and chooses me anyway, giving herself to me, letting me lose myself and be remade again and again in every curve of her body.

"That's it, baby. Take my cock, use it. It's yours, I'm yours. Fuck, Red." Her walls clamp against me and her leg wraps tighter around mine. I nearly lose my balance but catch myself so I can put my other hand under her ass, scooping her higher where she latches both legs around my hips instead.

Ginger reaches up and rips the blindfold off my eyes. She grabs at my arms, pulling herself up. I sit back on my feet and her hands land on my shoulders as she starts to ride me, taking what she needs just as I told her to. There are tear tracks running down her face and her beautiful hair is a wild halo around her, burning as bright as the fire that scorches the air between us.

She groans and pants, her body working in a sexy tango over mine. I'm completely lost to the sight of her taking her pleasure as her head drops back, exposing creamy inches of her neck to me. I wrap a hand loosely around her throat, my own grunts starting as my balls tighten and a heat stirs low in my groin. Her head snaps back into place and those wild eyes stare into my own, her pupils blown.

A renewed need rolls through me chanting its claim over her and my hands grip her hips, pulling her down harder with each thrust over my swollen cock. Her arms lock around my head, crushing me against her chest as her body quakes while she comes for a third time and I jump over the edge with her, my cock spasming with every pulse of her walls as it empties.

She relaxes her hold on me while her chest heaves and I grab her face, staring into those eyes that hold me captive, wiping her tears.

"You're a force," I tell her. She opens her mouth to speak, undeniably something snarky, and I silence her with my thumb on her lip, pulling it down. "A fucking hurricane, tearing through everything leaving total chaos in its wake. And the stronghold that's still standing after it's gone."

She searches my eyes, a moment of doubt living within her own.

"But that chaos leaves things raw, and fresh. I don't know what this is yet, Ginger. I don't know if you want the same things I do, and I don't care what you think you can or can't give me. I can't let you go. You've destroyed everything I thought I was and what's left here feels like something I've needed all along. I need this. I want this."

My hands move to her jaw as she leans in and locks her lips over mine. Her kiss is deep and soulful, touching something in each of us that's waking up from places we sent it to slumber that it can never go again.

CHAPTER SIXTEEN

Dane

The incessant buzzing from the table pulls me out of my sleep. I turn and glance over my shoulder, but Ginger isn't there.

"What?" I groan without even looking as I put the phone up to my ear.

"There's something we need to discuss. Why don't you join me in my ivory tower for breakfast."

I groan again at the sound of Jack's voice and pull the phone away from my ear to squint at the screen. It's seven a.m. which isn't usually problematic, but it was a long ass day yesterday, I've only been asleep for about three hours, and what I really want is to continue to sleep. I look around the room, it looks exactly the same as it did last night. There's no windows in here, which I suppose makes sense since the room is sandwiched between two others and the bed, and its frame of lights, take up most of the wall aside from the bookshelves. I squeeze the bridge of my nose and sigh.

"Yeah, okay. Give me a bit to catch a cab."

"Don't bother. James'll bring you."

The line goes dead, and I'm left staring at the ceiling wondering what discussion requires me to head to the office. The clothes I was wearing last night are draped over the bottom of the bed. I pull them on and wonder where Ginger got off to as I turn the knob and swing the door open. The hallway is as quiet as the room inside was, but I make my way back out to the right, headed for the doorway that's glowing red on the other side.

When I get to the front door, I reach a conundrum; I don't have keys for this one. Deciding I'm not left with much of a choice, I pull it closed behind me and make my way upstairs. I have no idea where James is, but he can come find me after I change into my own clothes.

Breakfast prep is in full swing when I make it into the apartment. The kitchen is bustling full of bodies getting ready for the day with the music up high and various stages of doneness on the counter. Bypassing the gathering, I make my way to my room and quickly change my clothes, stuffing the cash I brought with me back in my pocket. Who knows what I'm walking into; be prepared. I wish I could get the engrained lessons out of my head to stop feeding the unnecessary suspicion but there it is, gnawing at me.

I pass Michael in the hall as he's coming out of the bathroom, telling him about the unlocked door. Dude works downstairs, he must have a key. Assured it'll be handled, I give my teeth a brush and snag a muffin off the counter on my way back to the door, looking for Ginger and still not finding her. I stare at her door, the only one on this side of the apartment, wondering if she's in there. *If she left the bed last night after I was asleep and chose to sleep here instead...* There's an odd ache inside at the thought. The feelings I expressed are new for me, always discouraged as weakness by the men that raised us to follow them blindly.

The door to the apartment opens and shakes me out of my trance. James nods his head when I meet his eyes, and we head outside to a car waiting at the curb.

"Any idea what this is about?"

James grunts and doesn't bother to answer.

"Don't suppose you'll share?"

"Jack's had his eye on a few things happening. It looks like a few of his things are intertwined with a few of your things. And since you're here–"

He lets his thoughts drop off as he climbs in the car. There's no point in asking what once our seatbelts are locked in and we're off to talk to Jack anyway.

The ride through the city is long and busy. It's hard to imagine doing this every single day and I wonder how long I'll be able to stand it before I'm looking for a slow down again. Things start looking familiar as we reach the campus of the tech center Jack bought out from Adrian. It's the same as I remember it from when I was a kid; sprawling green lined in sculptures made from recycled materials, tables under trees, fountains in the intersections of walking paths. I remember this place well, it always seemed so free compared to the walls around the compound. Then suddenly the business was gone and so was the freedom I got to explore here.

James parks the car at the entryway and passes the keys off to a valet. That's new. We're escorted through doors bearing the Towertech logo by security and make our way up the glass elevator to the top floor. As the elevator goes up, I get peeks of people working, crowded around tables looking at things in various stages, rows of computers with employees in front of them, even what looks like a test firing range. When the elevator finally dings, it seems weird to be staring at a completely open space with just a desk and several couches in front of a wall of glass, considering the variety of bustling rooms we just breezed past.

Jack is on one of the couches next to a cart with covered dishes on it. We make our way across the room and James ushers me forward across from Jack before taking the seat beside me.

"Thanks for coming, guys."

He turns and grabs dishes off the cart, setting them in front of us and removing the lids. Poached eggs, bacon and fruit make up a wonderful aroma I'm eager to dig into. But first, "Why are we here?"

Jack finishes the bit he'd just placed in his mouth and wipes his lips with a napkin, clearing his throat. "Change of pace from my original plan. I received a rather disturbing letter and I'm not fucking amused."

He reaches into his pocket and pulls out a folded piece of paper, tossing it on the table and taking another bite. James picks it up, reading over it. His face turns stoney and he growls before he slams it down and looks at Jack.

"What are we doing about this?"

"What the fuck can I do? We don't have the manpower to take down a compound with counts we don't know and technology we're not aware of. We have runners on the inside, not guys who would know the kind of information we need. Clearly, as we've already seen." He looks at me pointedly.

I hold his glare and grab the letter for myself, scanning it. Russell has exact locations on Ginger, Ellen, Miriam, Jack's sister at their gran's house as well as his mom, and a list of other women I'm unfamiliar with. We're to return the women in seventy-two hours or the teams already in place will retaliate.

I run numbers in my head. "He doesn't have enough men to hit this many places at once and still protect the compound."

"Not in the compound, maybe. But what about other branches? I know of at least two smaller set ups further south. That's not to speak of the bigger compounds to the west. And what about Troy? Could they be working together?" All valid questions I wish I could answer for Jack.

The solution feels simple. I know it's not likely, but could it be? "Call them and tell them to pack and leave for a few days. Get on a plane, they can't follow them on an airplane."

"I'm going to assume everyone is bugged. As soon as Russell knows they're leaving, they'll be snatched. There's no way he'll let them get to the airport, much less on a plane." Jack's fingers are steepled over his mouth. He looks shook; it's completely unnerving.

"So, we send people in to extract them. Take them to the ski lodge with the others. How many men do you have?"

Jack huffs a laugh and sits back against the couch, arms out on the back of it. "The men we sent into the compound? That was all but two teams of them plus several favors I called in. I run a tech company and a small security firm. We do jobs protecting people. I'm not running a military style compound full of people eager to step in front of bullets for their twisted moment of glory."

"I have an idea," James cuts in.

The room is quiet while James pauses. Jack urges him on, and James blows out a long breath before he speaks. "Miriam and Ellen, they'd be expected to go do something together right? Especially so close to the baby coming. What if the three of them make plans to go somewhere we can extract all three at once? How many of the other women know each other? They could do something similar. We could get at least two sets of them out together before they figure out what we're doing. By then we can have teams ready to pull the rest simultaneously. I know a guy who has some guys."

"Of course you do," Jack quips and sighs. "I don't hate it. It could work."

"Too many moving pieces in seventy-two hours." Both men's attention snaps to me as I speak the obvious. "Especially if the clock was ticking when this letter came. How long has it been?"

"It was already here when I got in this morning, two hours ago. I called you immediately."

"Why me?"

"Because you started this mess. And because I need the possibility of even a little information if I'm looking for it and another body. Let's assume my phones aren't safe. James, call Damien and have him call Miriam and ask her if she wants to do the spa with Ellen tomorrow. If they're listening, they'll at least anticipate a change of venue tomorrow. Dane, go get Ginger on board. I need to start quietly collecting men and figure out how to get ahold of my sister and not tip anyone off. I may be taking a trip."

CHAPTER SEVENTEEN

Ginger

"This ain't good. How many women were on that list that we haven't heard from yet?" My nerves are fired up right now. Twelve names, twelve. All women I care about right down to Jack's mom, the sweet lady.

"There's concern that phones are bugged. We're trying to get ahold of people discreetly. That's why Miriam is inviting Ellen to the spa, and you should call and ask Ellen about her weekend plans and see if you can come."

"I don't like yer implications. I don't run from no one." My mind is spinning but my blood is running even hotter.

Dane stands, encasing me in his arms, his chin resting on my head. "Don't think of it like that. Think of it like helping us maximize the safety of two of the most important people you know. If all three of you are in the same place, it makes it easier to get them to safety and you'll be there to help."

"I think yer turnin' into a softie there, big guy."

He blows out a breath that sounds like a scoff. "You've got me all wrong. I'm just thinking about your big heart, babe. I wouldn't want to be on the other side of that fiery rage. I'm trying to save the poor assholes assigned to this job."

I swat at his chest as he laughs and think on it a minute. Really, I wouldn't want any sort of physical conflict to happen that Ellen might be on the receiving end of. That precious baby has been on my mind for months, getting to be her auntie has given me such a feeling of purpose and I love her already. "Yeah, okay. I'll go make the call."

"Good girl," he coos to my back, and I flip him the bird.

The phone rings, and rings, a few more times than I'm comfortable with. Ellen's voice beams at me through the phone with excitement when she does answer, apologizing that she was on the other line with Miriam. Perfect timing.

"That's no worries. Whatcha girls talkin' about?"

"She wants to go to the spa this weekend for a girl's day. A relaxing trip before the baby. Hey, what are you doing this weekend? I'd love for you to come and I'm sure Miriam wouldn't mind."

This almost feels too easy. It better not be too easy. "I was callin' ta see what yer doin' this weekend. Wanted to spend some girl time, too. The spa sounds amazin'. When were yous ladies thinkin'?"

"Tomorrow it sounds like. Miriam has the reservations all done up. She's going to come get me after breakfast. Want to come over tonight? Jack is out of town; we can veg and watch movies."

"You know it, girlie. Let me get the guys clued in on closin' up on their own and get some dinner in me and I'll be over. Don't eat all the popcorn before I get there."

We say our goodbyes and I tell Dane the plan. He sounds less than thrilled I'm changing locations and sleeping somewhere without the presence of seven men to come running if I scream. The upstairs apartment was designed for just that; to have defense if shit ever hit the fan and we got ambushed. It's why I sleep here, over the business, instead of somewhere away from the family I've built. This is one of the fan hitting times, and I'm intending to walk away from that protection and over to a townhouse that could very well be staked out.

"I'm coming with." Dane's arms are crossed, and he's got his no-nonsense face on.

"Didn't ya just call me a force less than twenty-four hours ago? Think I can handle it."

He cocks an eyebrow. "The last time you 'handled it' you almost got stabbed."

"I was distraught! I found a man I consida my brother layin' clocked out on the floor! And *you did* get stabbed, in case ya forgot. That's not reassuring."

He's silent and I watch his jaw tick. I've seen several sides of Dane in the few short weeks I've known him. I've seen a man determined enough to walk through fire. I've seen a man that turns soft when enamored by lust. I've seen a man quick to find solutions and clever enough for them to work. And I've seen this man, too. A man with impenetrable walls and rage beating on the other side like a bull trying to get through.

"I'm going. You and me? This isn't a democracy. Just because you don't want something doesn't mean I'll okay-darling you and give in. Not if it means I have to sit here on my ass and picture the fifty different ways you could be hurting, or worse. Fuck that noise, I'm coming."

We're on either side of the table between us in a standoff, neither willing to break the stare down we've created. The implication of what he's saying hits me and it hits me hard. At a young age, I built all of this against all the odds stacked against me. This family I've brought together, each one seeking a better way, having come from something so broken that it was breaking them. This place is about salvation in more ways than one.

While I assess Dane, I can see clearly that he's not so different from the rest. His whole life was broken, raised in a way of thinking that's so extreme it forced his hand to break it in return. How he grew up in the environment that he did and came out the other end wanting to flip it on its head, is astounding in a way that only the broken can understand. And so maybe, if I remember that place that I came from, remember that woman desperate to protect herself and let her see it, I can relent on this, if only to give him a shred of the peace he's always been missing.

"Okay. But it's not like ya can come waltzin' through the front door. You'll hafta get creative."

He grins that wicked grin that makes my toes curl a little and his arms uncross to fall to his sides. "Creative I can do, Red."

CHAPTER EIGHTEEN

Dane

In the end, I convinced Michael and his roommate Richie to ride with me and camp out at Jack and Ellen's. I had considered Damien and Alex to be the ideal choice, but their women's names were on the list and I'm positive they're home with the doors locked and on high alert. In the grand scheme of things, it turns out that each of the men that left the compound with Jack years ago, had someone on that list. Our insane fathers had been watching them the whole time, hibernating until the time was right. And as it sits, that time is when we stole from them what they wanted most of all; future generations.

The "creative" part of our entrance is where we get stuck. We take the town car and Michael drops Ellen off at the end of Jack's driveway as Richie and I stay put in the back with the dark tint. We watch her go up the walk the same way the guy camped across the street slunk down in his driver's seat watches her. It takes everything in me not to get out of the car and use his own gun to put two between his eyes. The rational part of my brain wins out with the argument that initiating more violence won't help us. *Levelheaded bastard.*

So, we drive back to Ginger's while watching the whole way for a tail and trade the town car for Michael's Jeep and drive back to the townhouse, choosing to park three streets behind it and praying the neighbors behind him don't have security cameras or dogs.

Michael leads the way as we get out of the car, checking the street for more parked cars and peeking around the first house. "No fence," he whispers, and we step off the sidewalk to follow him.

"Stay low," I warn them both. The last thing we need is someone seeing us slink past their windows and calling in the police. Especially not knowing if the responders that come would be actual police or hired thugs.

House one cleared, we move into the second yard too quickly and a flood light tucked high into a corner illuminates the space in front of us. Michael curses and we all push back behind the tree in the yard we came from before moving one house over. There's a for sale sign by the curb that's reassuring, when coupled with the empty driveway next to the house, and the line of thin cypress trees lining the other side, blocking us from their neighbors.

Crossing the street proves more difficult. We come out under a streetlight and there are two cars parked a few houses down, both occupied. It wouldn't be unlike Russell to put guys behind a target where they're less obvious. The house they're in front of is directly behind Jack's, giving an easy in if they're needed.

Never one to linger too long on an issue, I smack the back of my hand across Richie's chest and laugh a little louder than necessary as I turn in the opposite direction and start walking. Neither man misses a beat and fall in step behind me, smiling and chatting nonsensically. To anyone who doesn't recognize us, we're out for a stroll. I doubt anyone noticed where we came in carefully and slowly out of the driveway. When I'm sure we are far enough away to disappear again I casually step into the driveway of a dark house and keep walking quickly up the driveway.

"That's not good." Richie looks concerned, and rightfully so.

"Did you guys see more than one car in front of the house?" I call up all the cars parked on the street, but I really don't think I saw more than one person.

"No, but it doesn't mean they didn't find other places to hide."

"One problem at a time, I guess. We have to actually get to the house." I peek my head around the corner, noting the fence in the neighbor's yard. I'm glad I didn't pick that yard but pissed we have to work around it. The house behind it has a lower fence, more for aesthetic than function and I pick that one, relieved when no lights turn on or dogs sound. But my triumph is short lived when I hear a gun cock at the same time I hear an *umph* behind me and everything goes black.

***

When I come to, I'm dripping in ice cold water. It takes me a minute to orient myself. I'm in a vault room in the compound judging by the sterile room with no windows and steel door in front of me. I'm also tied to a fucking chair. Great. Russell sits in front of me with the bucket still in his hands and a pissed off expression on his face.

"There he is. Welcome back to the world of the living."

There's a whimper and I turn to the right to see Ginger also tied to a chair and gagged, which means she gave them hell. I silently applaud her and look back at Russell almost immediately. Showing any concern or recognition would put us in a more precarious situation than the one we're already in.

"Fuck off." I spit the blood I taste in my mouth at his feet. It'll get me in a load of shit, but hopefully it'll keep his attention on me.

He tsks and shakes his head. The man I didn't realize was behind me cuffs me across the side of my head and I work hard to look unphased even though my head swims. I focus on the specks of gold twinkling in the tiles on the floor.

"Let's try that again." Russell's voice comes out cool and calculated.

"Where are the other guys I was with?" Unless they're behind me, too, they aren't in this room. Ginger's breathing sounds panicked. I want to look to make sure she's okay, but I'm still focused on not drawing attention to her.

"Left where they were found. It's not them I want. I imagine the nice old lady that lives in the yard you invaded will find them if they don't wake up on their own. Where are my women?"

I bring my gaze up to meet his, rage burning inside me. I'm certain it shows because Russell stands with a chuckle.

"Ah, Dane. Always the hero, aren't you? It's a fatal flaw, you know? Being the hero instead of falling in line. It's why you could never be trusted, even when you were small. Always swooping in to steal someone else's beating, always taking the fall for the smaller kids when we knew damn well you didn't do something you were taking credit for. Look where being the hero has gotten you."

Ginger squeals and I risk looking at her. Shelton, damn military follow along, has her by her hair. Her head is pulled back tight, her neck exposed. She's gasping for air and her eyes are huge.

I try to control my voice, bringing it as steady as my hammering heart will allow. "Leave the lady out of it. She didn't have anything to do with anything."

Russell moves around into my line of sight, blocking Ginger from my view. She squeaks again and I do my best not to flinch at the sound. "Well, that's going to be a problem, you see. Because that bitch over there has been keeping Jack busy for years along with housing all the guys that have left their responsibilities here. And I have it on pretty good authority she put up quite the show to earn a rather large property that sure looks like it's getting ready to house a rather large group of people. And–" He pulls his phone out of his pocket and calls up a photo, turning it to face me. "It sure looks to me like this is you buying that property with money I know you don't have."

He swipes to the left and another photo from outside the apartment complex pops up. "And it sure looks to me like Jack and that bitch are working on that property together."

Russell steps forward, closing his hand over my throat and squeezing. He waits, watching as my breathing gets shallower the harder he squeezes. When it feels like I can barely get any breath in, I draw slowly through my nose and hold it.

"So, I'll ask you again." His voice drops low, and his face comes close as my lungs start burning. "Where are my women?"

I focus on the flash of Ginger's bright hair that I can see over Russell's head, ignoring the malice on his face as he stares me down. A trickle of sweat starts making its way over the side of my face, or blood, I don't know which. I ignore it and stay focused on Ginger's hair and the sound of her breathing until I can't hold that breath anymore.

"You'll never find them," I choke out. Russell gives me a shake and pushes me backward before he storms off. I sputter out the breath left in my lungs and gasp for fresh air.

Russell stalks back our way with a knife and a blowtorch in his hand. "Maybe I won't find them. But when they find her, they'll need to pull teeth to figure out who she is." He sneers at me and sets the blowtorch on the table next to us, lighting it up and sticking the knife in it. Ginger starts screaming against the gag in her mouth and I rock my chair in an attempt to loosen the ties.

"Leave her alone, Russell. She doesn't know anything; she was just doing Jack a favor. It's me you want; she can't help you."

"I think she can. See I've seen you going in and out of her business with my own two eyes. I think she can help me loosen your tongue, boy. And no one cares about her. Your daddy would be awfully mad at me if I messed you up though. He wants you back so you can carry on his line."

Seemingly satisfied with the color of his blade, he shuts off the torch and points it at Ginger's face. "Where are my women?" he asks again.

I yank at my hands, feeling my skin tearing and not caring. The knot budges, but not enough to help me at all. "Leave her alone. Let her go and I'll come back. I'll help you recruit."

"That's not what I asked you, boy." Russell touches the knife to Ginger's bare upper arm and she screams. The sound tears through my system and sets everything on edge. The terror behind it awakens a primal instinct deep inside of me and I swear my vision turns red.

"You son of–" The overhead system drowns out the rest of my words as alarms scream and the lights flicker.

Russell freezes for a few moments and I see the opening I need. Picking the chair up from underneath me I run backwards to the wall and slam into it as hard as I can.

The shock of the chair against the wall jolts me but all it does is crack; not enough. Russell's goon comes rushing my way, but I don't have time to worry about him as Russell smiles and takes up a position behind Ginger, holding her head in place to watch me while tears stream down her face.

I turn my side to the wall and slam into it again, and again and then Shelton is rearing back, ready to punch me. I duck and he stumbles into the space I was in. The sudden movement takes me off my feet as I lose my balance to the chair on my back. It's difficult, but I push back to a stand and bend forward, rushing Shelton and slamming my shoulder into his gut. Unexpecting of my intent, he takes the impact and we both tumble to the ground. I roll off him and rush the wall again, this time managing to snap the chair. I feel one chair arm come loose and swing it around in an attempt to break it the rest of the way off. Shelton recovers too fast, and I curse as he connects a fist with my gut.

"Here's where he's going to lose it, sweetheart. Because he's too cocky. Here's where we'll get to play." I turn in time to see Russell lick a path up Ginger's cheek and she cringes, a sob coming through her gag. She's trying to wrestle her head out of his grasp but failing with the way she's tied around the chest to the chair with her hands behind her. If I can manage to get free, I'll have to kill both of these men to get her out.

The sirens still blaring over us reminding everyone there's an intruder somewhere. I come back to my feet and Shelton chuckles darkly. "Give it up, Dane. What do you think you can possibly do here?"

"This," is my reply as I bring my knee up into his groin. It's a cheap shot, but it's effective. He scrunches in on himself and I bring my knee up again as hard I can into his face. A sickening crack gives me the satisfaction of knowing when he hits the ground this time, it'll be a while before he gets back up. I slam myself against the wall one more time and my arms break free. Granted they're each still attached to the chair, but I can pull them in front of me.

I grab a chair side to brandish it as a weapon and freeze. Russell has one hand full of Ginger's hair, and the other with the still faintly glowing knife hovering over her neck.

"Tell me, Dane. If I were to cut her throat with a hot knife, do you think it would cauterize it as I go and give her more time? Or do you think she'd bleed out faster from the burn?"

"Tell me, Russell. If I impale you on this chair, do you think it'll hurt when I drag your bleeding body down the hallway with me?"

"Who do you think is faster?" He presses the knife tip to Ginger's throat, and she winces, breathing heavy through the gag but not daring to make a sound. Her flesh turns bright red, and I do the only thing I can think; I call his bluff and surprise him at the same time, swinging one leg out to sweep the chair from under Ginger's weight as I throw the other arm and chair half against him.

I dive forward as my arm connects with Russell, hoping to use any part of me to break Ginger's fall so she doesn't bash her head against the concrete floor. Russell falls backward with an oomph, clattering against the table and I barely get an arm under Ginger.

Russell pushes himself off the table and switches hands with the knife, barreling forward toward us. I kick my feet up and shove him back before scrambling up to my feet. He lunges for me but misses and I get him in the face with an elbow, turning as he circles so Ginger doesn't get caught in the mix. He swipes at me, and I jump back, and then again, narrowly avoiding the tip of his blade the second time.

When he takes a swipe at me a third time, I grab his wrist and pull, propelling him forward with a crash into the wall where he trips over Shelton's still unconscious body. He drops the knife in an effort to catch himself and when he stoops slightly to pick it up, I wind up and punt him in the head. He sputters for a second, and wobbles slightly like he's straight out of a cartoon, then crumples forward in a heap next to Shelton.

I'm standing awkwardly in disbelief when I hear an irritated sound from behind me. Ginger is struggling against the ropes tying her to the chair, her head cocked to the side from the way she's slumped in the overturned seat. I grab the discarded knife and squat behind the chair to cut at the ropes. It feels like it takes hours instead of minutes, and I keep expecting someone to come bursting through the door. Either no one knows we're down here, or they've been instructed to stay clear.

I'm just getting through the ropes when Shelton starts to groan. I saw faster, watching him shake his head and moan again. Ginger starts squeaking and I stop for a second to pull the gag out of her mouth.

"Hurry!" she cries.

"I'm trying, babe. Are you okay?"

"I'll be betta when we're far away from this place." Shelton is rolling to his side now, too close to coherent for my comfort. My body aches when I come back to standing so I can give him another hearty kick before returning to my task.

"Agreed. Where's Ellen?" If she's here and we leave without her, Jack will never forgive me. If Jack isn't already here and the cause for the siren still giving me a headache.

"Hopefully still in the panic room. Those knuckleheads caught me at the bedroom door, and I watched her close herself in."

"Thank God for small favors," I mumble as the rope breaks free and Ginger begins to tug at the ones around her chest. She pushes them over her head, wiggling out from under them and all but throws herself into my arms.

She's shaking as she holds me, and while I'd love to stay in this moment, we truly aren't safe yet. I hold her at arm's length and inspect her again. The burn on her throat is bubbled and angry looking, but she looks okay otherwise. I hand her a piece of the chair still attached to my arms by the rope.

"Hold this steady," I instruct, and begin the sawing process to free myself all over again.

CHAPTER NINETEEN

Ginger

By the time Dane gets himself free of the chair he splintered into pieces, the sirens have stopped but the lights are still flashing, and a deeper tone is sounding somewhere in the distance. I can't tell if it's inside or outside of the building we're in, if you could call a complete structure buried inside the soil a building.

When they brought us here, we entered a garage at street level and took an elevator down, and down, and down. In this building, we're literally underground.

Dane being out for so long was unnerving. His uncle staring a hole through me was more unnerving. And having heard of so much photographic evidence against us, I have an extremely unsettled feeling in my gut. Unsettled and violated.

Dane checks the room over for anything he can use other than the knife and comes up empty. "We're going to have to go slow and quiet. Whatever is going on up there is bound to have people distracted, but that doesn't mean we're safe. Got it?"

"I'm not a child, Dane. I can do hard things and assess danger."

A chuckle gets cut off as he shakes his head before turning to the door and pulling me along behind him. "Knife to her throat ten minutes ago and she's still spitting fire at me."

Dane cracks the door and peeks into the hallway. The deeper alarm sound gets louder, suggesting it's coming from inside the building after all. After looking both ways several times, he gives my hand a squeeze and we move into the hall. He pulls me into his back and slides tight against the wall as we work around the curve of the hallway toward the orange flashing light coming from around the corner.

The air around us feels thick, whether it's poor ventilation down this far or my own lack of oxygen from the trauma we left back in the room, I'm not sure. I try to take a few steadying breaths as Dane leads us further down the hall.

We round a corner to the left at a split rather than crossing over to the right and the buzzing noise gets louder before slowly dropping off again. Dane freezes. It's not lost on me that the sudden increase and drop off is most likely a door opening somewhere on this level. I strain to hear any indication we're no longer alone, but the droning buzzer drowns out everything else in this never-ending maze of a concrete hallway.

Dane flattens his back against the wall and leans into me. "We have to keep moving. Stay close and try not to make any noise."

"When they drove us in, we crossed over the river. Is there a feed fer it somewheres in here?"

He contemplates my question for several moments, his brows pinched in concentration. "It's not like the storm systems we came in before. There's a water intake closer to the ground level built into the mouth of a cave, it used to be a boat launch before they built the compound. It would be better than trying to get over the fence around the back perimeter. But it's locked up, I don't know if we can get through."

"Yer nutso if you think I'm gonna stand around here and wait ta see what happens next. Let's go find us a water intake, doll."

Dane grunts and looks around like he needs to orient himself in the hallway that only stretches left and right before turning to the right. He creeps to the edge of the wall and looks back the way we came then ushers me across the opening, following behind me.

"That door up there, it's for a staircase. Do you know what level we're on?"

"I wasn't exactly doin' no countin', Dane. I was busy worryin' about whether or not you were breathin'."

"Can you make a guess?" I have to hand it to him; he doesn't sound as irritated as I feel right now with my head pounding and the incessant buzzing getting louder.

"I don't know. The elevator dinged ten, maybe twelve times. Why does it matta? We're goin' up either way, right?"

He sighs and looks at the ceiling. I can see him working to keep his cool. "There's no floor indicators in this building. If you give an enemy a point of reference, it's easier for them to find you. If you disorient them, it's easier to defend."

"Oh." *Well, that settles that then.*

Dane scoots in front of me again when we reach the door, tucking me tight against the wall and peering into the corner of a small window on it. He turns his head after a second, looking up into the stairwell. He slowly pushes the handle down and swings the door open, waiting before moving into the open entryway and grabbing my hand to follow him through.

The door bangs loudly behind us, something I hadn't anticipated when I left it to close and Dane springs into action, pulling me quickly up the first set of stairs. We reach the top of the second set of stairs when the door bangs open behind us.

"Up or down?" someone shouts.

"You guys take down, we'll go up," another voice answers.

Dane turns and looks at me and I feel the panic on my face. He pushes me ahead of him toward the next set of stairs. "Keep going," he urges.

Up and up we go with footsteps pounding on the stairs behind us and the ever present alarm sounding over us. My thighs begin to ache when I count the sixth staircase and my breathing is becoming labored, the air burning on its way in. I push myself harder, hoping my guess of ten was accurate and we're more than halfway there.

"Two more then we duck in a door and hope they're far enough behind us they have to split up again," I hear Dane say low behind me.

We pass one door and turn again to the next set of eleven stairs. Each level, exactly eleven stairs, then a landing that's eight paces wide. When I crest the last stair I lunge for the door, yanking it open and collapsing against the wall, my breath coming out in gasps as Dane carefully pulls the handle down and pushes the door closed, then presses himself flat against the wall, his hand on his lips in a gesture of silence.

I count the seconds up in my head while I try to control my breathing; seventeen, eighteen. A shadow passes on the wall in front of me, then another only seconds behind it, then the wall illuminates again with the light from the hallway.

I watch Dane, his breathing even in a way I wish mine could be, his fingers pressed firmly into the wall behind him, ready to spring forward at any moment.

"Now what?" I ask him. "We can't exactly go back out there, can we?"

His fingers press into his forehead, and I can practically see the wheels in his head turning. "There's a food delivery access elevator, runs from the ground level to level nine where the kitchen is. We're definitely up far enough for that. We could ride it up, we just have to hope there's no one there waiting."

Decided, he takes my hand and leads me down yet another rounded hallway that seems to never end until we reach another left or right option. Heading right, we face a narrow silver door. Dane pushes the button and after a minute and much impatience, it makes a loud ding.

The inside is tight, clearly not built for much more than a body and a cart. Dane pushes the third button from the top and the door closes again, creaking before it begins moving up.

As quickly as it started, the elevator slows to a halt. It seems like we could've made it one more set of stairs and would have been where we needed to be. Now we chance someone waiting for us. My breath quickens and Dane squeezes my hand.

"We're fine," he soothes. "They'd assume we went all the way up to leave through the garage, not stop on the third floor."

The door opens, revealing the distant sound of gunfire. If we're only two floors from the surface, what's going on out there?

Dane quickly leads the way into the hallway, pushing me behind him again so he can look around the corner. He lingers a second and then jolts back. A second later a bullet lodges in the wall opposite of us.

"Back in tha elevator?" I ask.

Dane shakes his head and turns, putting me in the front position along the wall. "Ready? You're gonna run. No looking, no waiting. I'm going to count and you're going to bolt, got it?"

"Why me first?"

"Because they won't be ready. Once you're across, they're going to watch closer or start coming at us. Run, and don't stop, I'll be right behind you."

I'm unsure of this plan. It feels like he's trying to get himself killed, again. But he's staring deep into me, and I can feel the plea in his eyes.

"One."

"Dane."

"Two."

"Please," I whisper.

"Three."

He spins me around, kisses my shoulder and pushes me. I don't wait, I don't hesitate, the second one foot is out front, I run. I hear the gun go off again and the bullets lodge in the wall to my right. I want to look, I want to make sure Dane is behind me where he said he'd be as more gunshots ring out, and especially as I hear a grunt behind me.

Inside the building, the bangs are loud, ringing over the alarm that's blaring at this level and though I can't hear it, I whimper. My mind goes to Ellen and even in this moment, I can't help but hope she locked the door on that panic room and never came out.

I shriek when a hand lands on my elbow but as I turn, I see it's Dane's hand. "Faster," he urges, panic in his eyes. I don't want to know what put it there, I just lean forward a little and force my legs to carry me faster.

Dane steers me around the curve of the hallway, and then to the right. At the end of the hallway is another door, this one wood with a window over the top of it. Dane turns the handle, but it doesn't budge. He throws his shoulder against the door and curses. His gaze moves to the window over the door.

He looks around the hallway and then jogs quickly a few doors down, bringing back a small fire extinguisher. He pushes me behind him and sizes up the fire extinguisher, glancing between it and the space over the door before he rears back and throws it into the window.

The crashing noise of the glass is jarring and worrisome. If the men behind us before hadn't figured out where we went, they're going to know now.

"Up," Dane demands, squatting down with his fingers threaded together.

"Ya can't be serious," I squeak.

"I don't have the time to argue with you right now, Red. You need to go through the window and open the door from the other side so we can get the hell out of here. Put your foot in my hand so I can boost you up."

"You don't need to be an ass!"

"You need to learn to listen sometimes."

"It's high." My voice comes out soft and his features fall.

Dane puts a hand on each side of my face. "Listen to me, Ginger. I've got you, okay? Put your foot in my hand

and your hands on my shoulders. I'll boost you up, you grab the windowsill and make sure to be careful of the glass. I'll help push your legs up, okay? Turn around and drop to the other side. It's only a few feet higher than you are. You need to save us. Can you save me, Ginger?"

His words hit me in the chest. I look at him and see the man that he is, but I see the boy he was not that long ago, too, scared and wishing for a different life. A life he took into his own hands and used to save several dozen women and children. Redemption for all the years he was too afraid to do anything but listen. Now it's my turn. I nod my head.

"Good girl," he says, linking his hands back together and bending forward once again.

I secure my foot in his hands and stop. He looks up, inquisitive, and I place a single kiss on his lips. "Don't you die on me before I get that door open. I mean it."

"Yes ma'am." He smiles.

I put my hands on his shoulders, and he gives me a little bounce, testing my weight, before he boosts me up. I use the hem of my shirt to clear the broken glass from the ledge and grab hold. Dane pushes and I get my elbows up, wrapping my arms over the ledge so I can haul myself up higher. I hear shouting and Dane pushes again, much more insistently. I've got one knee to the ledge when he lets go of my other foot and I hear the sound of flesh on flesh.

"Dane?"

"Get inside!" he yells through the noise of what is clearly a ringer going on under me.

Someone swipes for my foot and misses, and I scramble to get my leg over the ledge so I can drop down inside. Once my feet are back on the floor, I hesitate. If he's losing the fight on the other side of the door and I open it, there's no way I can take on multiple men with guns.

I turn into the space I just entered. It's dark, but as my eyes adjust, I can see sporting equipment on the walls, boat oars hanging next to it, a sauna, and I'm pretty sure that's a liquor cabinet. It's a funny array of things, but I can work with this.

Grabbing a pair of baseball bats I hustle to the door. There are two different deadbolts, must be why Dane couldn't get it to budge. Grunting comes from the other side of the door as I turn the locks and grip the handle. I take a breath in through my nose and pointedly exhale it through pursed lips, turn the handle, and swing open the door.

The hallway looks like something straight out of a low budget flick. There are three guys laid out on the floor, and another has Dane in a headlock. They're both sweaty and there's blood running down the side of the guy's head almost the same color as the blood I hadn't noticed before soaking through the arm of Dane's shirt.

The man holding Dane looks up at me and makes a growling sound, reinforcing the hold he has on Dane.

"Alright, asshole," I say, dropping one bat and swinging the remaining one around in my hand. The grin on my face feels maniacal as I take a step forward, rear the bat back and take aim.

Mr. Headlock has the good sense to look worried for a second and loosen his hold on Dane. I swing and he jumps back, allowing Dane to break free and sputter for breath as my bat breaks the air where his head should have been. Pulling the bat back into position, I move forward into the space he just occupied, our violent dance following the tempo of my hammering heart.

"I should tell ya'; I was the captain of my softball team. We only eva lost one game."

He grins like he's trying not to laugh at my apparent joke and his eyes track behind me. I take the distraction and charge him, swinging again when I get close enough. He reaches out at the last moment and grabs the end of the bat, halting my momentum. It's of no concern, though. Swinging a bat isn't my only talent. While he's busy grinning about the bat in his hand, I pull back my foot and bury it in his gut. He hunches over with a cry, right where I want him so I can bring my foot back again and knee him in the face, just like I watched Dane do.

Mr. Headlock goes down like a ton of bricks, and I pull my bat free from his hold.

"I came to help, but I see that wasn't necessary," Dane says from beside me. He's still breathing too hard and has a hand pressed over his bicep.

"You alright?" I try to pry his hand off his arm, but he grunts and turns it away from me.

"Not right now. We gotta go. Come on."

I take a sweeping look over the hallway again before quickly following Dane through the doorway back into the room we busted into and lock the door behind me. I find him at a counter tearing through a cabinet.

"Whatcha doin'?"

"I need gauze, or rags, or something." Finished with that cabinet, he opens the one next to it and I open the one on the other side.

"How 'bout these?" I ask, pulling out a pile of neatly folded white shirts from their spot beside bottles of dyes. This has to be a recreational storage room, there's simply too many oddball things in here and I wonder what else we might find if we took the time to explore.

"Perfect." He takes the shirt from the top of the stack and wraps it around his arm, pulling it tight and making a knot over the top before taking another shirt and stuffing it underneath.

"Gonna tell me what happened?"

"I didn't make it through the hallway, got grazed. No big deal." The way he says it so casually makes my blood boil.

"No big deal? You got shot! First, ya get stabbed, and now ya got shot?"

"You forgot where we both got kidnapped. Help me tear these up and stop worrying about my arm." Dane is focused as he busts the seam of a shirt and starts tearing off strips. He gets a few good-sized ones from the shirt before he hands it to me to finish up.

When he's finished with the second shirt he picked up he stalks quickly across the room, clearly on a mission. When he reaches the liquor cabinet he wraps his hand in some of the fabric and smashes his fist through the glass front, grabbing several bottles on his way out of it.

"Pain relief?" I tease.

"More like therapy," he deadpans.

I tilt my head, confused. Dane unscrews the bottles he pulled out and stuffs fabric into the tops before grabbing several more bottles and doing the same.

"Open the door, would ya, babe?" he asks, pulling a lighter out of his pocket. It occurs to me what his plan is, and my eyebrows shoot up as I rush ahead of him to the door.

The men on the floor outside the door are rousing. Dane doesn't waste any time, lighting up two bottles and throwing them down the hallway before doing the same on the other side. He picks up the last bottle and splashes it on the walls around us before he flicks open the lighter in his hand and lights the flame.

"The door out to the water intake is through the door in the far left corner of the room behind us. Head that way. Now." His voice is calm, too calm, and completely steady.

"Fuckin' moonshiners," he mutters. I watch as he fills his mouth with liquor before he looks at me and nods his head behind us, silently instructing me again to move.

I walk backwards and watch him stand up a little straighter, then he blows the liquor through the flame of the lighter. The space in front of him fills with a flash of fire and the walls catch. Dane casually tosses the lighter to the floor and backs up into the room, closing the door behind him once more. As he turns and takes several steps in my direction, the empty window space above his head shines orange and smoke begins to roll in. Dane stalks through the room with a determined look on his face and a bat back in his hand, a man hellbent on revenge.

CHAPTER TWENTY

Dane

When I reach Ginger, I turn her around and urge her to move. The shocked look on her face is punctuated by the moonshine still burning in my mouth. I never did like that stuff, but it's useful for a few things; like sending this place back to hell where it belongs.

Side by side we walk through the door at the back of the room and enter the short hall to the secondary door that will lead us out into the intake and the fresh air. With any luck, there'll be a boat there still, but I fully anticipate it'll be empty after the last time we were all caught partying on the river. As long as it hasn't been bricked up, I don't really care.

We pass several other closed doors marked with standard things this far back into the vault; boiler room, janitorial, dry storage. Then we arrive. I spot the padlock on the outside of the door and the anger I'd just dispelled when I lit the hallway up, boils back to the surface. I mimic

Ginger's anger the night of the auction and put my fist in the wall.

"Hey! Come'on, hey!" She closes her hand over mine before I can put it through again.

"This is bullshit! Tied up, shot, jumped in a fucking hallway outside a locked door, a goddamn padlock." I point to the offending lock and grab Ginger, both hands on her face, cradling her jaw. I touch my forehead to hers and take a shuddering breath as my eyes close. "I just want to get you out of here."

Her hands find my face in the same manner before they slide backwards and cup around my neck. Her thumbs rub slow circles in the hollows under my ears and I feel the tension coiled in my body give way a little.

"Take a deep breath and think on it. There's gotta be somethin' around here that can help, right? How do you get through a lock?" Her voice is soft, coaxing me into a calm.

"Shouldn't I ask you that? With all that gear you were playing with earlier I would think you'd be the badass that could bust through locks."

She gives a soft huff that comes out a little like a snort and my grin spreads. As I let myself get lost in the feel of her hands a thought pops into my head. A bit of a video I watched once that I dismissed as bullshit. But anything is worth a shot.

Disentangling myself from Ginger, I make my way into the janitor's closet, praying there's wrenches in here. It takes me a few minutes digging through shelves to unearth a toolkit but I'm in luck when I find several wrenches.

I emerge from the closet and Ginger gives me a strange look but follows me curiously. "I saw this once. Don't have any idea if it works, but I guess we'll find out."

I slot one wrench over each of the bars on the padlock, touching the sides of the heads together, then slowly press my hands together. The tension is intense, and they don't want to slide together any further.

"Come on," I coax them. "Do it for me, sweetheart." I press a little harder and feel the lock give just a little. Gritting my teeth, I engage my shoulders and push. The side of the lock snaps, plastic flying into the wall and my hands jarring together as the tension releases.

A shocked laugh bubbles out of Ginger, and she smiles as I tear the lock off the door and pull it open. We run through into the darkness. However long has passed since we've been here, it isn't dawn just yet. The low light will make a good cover when we're clear of the river.

We rush down the concrete path running through the tunnel walls along the river. I'm pretty sure no one is following us through the fire and the locked doors, but I'm also not willing to find out. When the mouth of the tunnel opens up and the path turns into a pier, I realize what I worried about from the start; there's no boats here.

"Can you swim?" I ask Ginger.

"I can not-drown, if that counts fer anythin'."

"It'll have to."

I climb over the railing onto the narrow ledge and turn to help Ginger over. We stand together, hands clasped, and I look over at her. The last of the moonlight and the bit of light blue starting in the sky highlights her high cheek bones and the tip of her nose. Her hair blows in the wind, tinted blue like the rest of the light around us. I lean into her, and she meets me in a gentle but lingering kiss.

"Ready?" I ask. She nods her head, and her bottom lip gets caught in her teeth.

"Promise ya won't let me drown, okay?" She looks nervous and I wonder where not-drowning meets actual swimming as I nod my head.

"I've got you, Red. I've always got you."

She squeezes my hand, and I let go to jump into the water. It's an ice-cold shock to my system but I break the surface and reach for her anyway. She looks around nervously and then jumps in after me, plugging her nose and creating a sight I try hard not to laugh at.

She sputters up and I pull her into my side. Slowly, we fall into a rhythm and work our way down the river. I do my best to stay low over the surface and Ginger just barely stays afloat. After a while she stops trying to swim and just frog kicks. Her breaths are coming in bigger gasps, and I can tell she's wearing out.

"Just a little bit further and it'll open into the lake, I promise. We can go up the bank a little and disappear into the woods on the other side."

Ginger nods, her lips quivering, then focuses in front of us again as she pushes her body to slice through more cold water. The trees thin out several minutes later and the current grabs us, ready to push us into the lake over the tiny five-foot falls. I send up a silent thank you to the universe and pull Ginger into me again. I tread water with one arm as I secure her to me with the other and tell her to be ready for a small drop as I kick to keep us moving forward. I've done this a hundred times every summer. It's cold out now, but it won't be any different. Easy drop, kick up, swim to shore.

The falls suck us over and Ginger squeals as we fall the short distance, cannonballing into the bubbly water below. I orient myself and kick to the surface, dragging a flailing Ginger with me. We turn to the right and make our way down the embankment and then up to the beach. The sun is cresting on the horizon when our feet hit sand at the bottom of the lake, and we begin trudging our way out of the water.

The water reaches my shins when Ginger tugs on my arm. I spin to face her, and she leaps forward. I'm barely able to catch her as her lips crash into mine. She's shivering and her breaths come in hiccups, but she dives back at my mouth again and again. My tired limbs can't hold her, and I sit in the water only to have her climb over me, pushing me down. The waves wash around us as she comes in for more. I become lost in the tangle of our tongues and the rush of the water over my skin until my own body starts shaking from the cold.

"There's an old hunting cabin about a quarter mile into the woods. We can't start a fire, but there's blankets and dry clothes."

"And a bed? Tell me there's a bed. I'm exhausted."

I grin because I can. Because we're alive to have this conversation. "There's a bed. I'll keep watch."

When our feet hit dry sand, I could fall to the ground and kiss it. Ginger mumbles her gratitude and we make our way up the beach toward the trees. Halfway there, Ginger stops and points.

"That's a whole lotta smoke."

"Good. Let the whole damn compound burn. Good riddance."

"Dane, that's yer dad in there, yer uncle, people ya grew up with. Yer whole past is goin' up in flames. Bein' exchanged fer a future that's uncertain. Ya can't go back from that. You sure yer okay with the consequences of that?"

Her gaze is one of absolute worry. Like she's trying to add up the bill of my life's story and coming up short. The truth is, I don't want to go back any more than I would want to round up all the people we stole in the cover of night and flashed an opportunity in front of. There's nothing inside those walls that matters to me. The men inside are a stain on my soul I'm not sure I can ever scrub free no matter how hard I try. And I'm moving forward. That means protecting the people I care about who are willing to take a chance on me as well. That means giving everything I have to her for as long as she'll allow me.

"The cost is unimportant, Red. I'll shelter you even if it costs me everything. I'll burn the whole city down to keep you standing. They wanted to make an example out of you, so I made one of them instead. I don't want anything that's been touched by them. I just want you."

Her expression softens and her eyes well with tears. She looks up into the sky, blinking to stop them from falling and her breath hitches. I wrap my arms around her, one hand stroking the wet hair clinging to her scalp. Her bravado breaks and she sobs into my chest. We stand there on the sand as the sun comes up, wrapped in each other, sharing body heat until her tears slow.

When her breathing levels out, I press a kiss to the top of her head, thankful that everyone will be too preoccupied with the fire to bother looking for us. "Come on. Let's go get warm."

CHAPTER TWENTY ONE

Ginger

There's no sunlight streaming in the room when I wake up. There's no windows in this place. Dane called it a cabin, but it's set back into the hills and disguised to blend in. He doesn't know where it came from, only that it's always been empty, and he's kept it stocked with clothes and supplies since he was a teenager.

The walls inside are smooth, worn brick and lit with sconces in the center of each one. There's no overhead lights, and there's no heat aside from a fire burning stove so the air is chilled. But he was right, there's a massive pile of blankets nested around me and our shared body heat in our fresh clothes was plenty enough to keep me warm while I drifted off.

My eyes land on Dane trying to quietly close the creaky front door, very likely what woke me up. He's covered in a fine sheen of sweat and his red checkered shirt is open, revealing a damp white shirt underneath. Now that I'm rested, he looks like quite a treat.

"Sorry," he whispers. "Did I wake you up?"

"I'm fine," I reply, stretching. "I feel pretty good. Did you get any sleep in?"

A soft moan leaves him as he tracks my movements. "A few hours, at least. Enough to be able to make it up the peak with the satellite phone. Damien is on his way to get us. Should be about an hour. They were looking for us last night before I set the place on fire."

Dane grabs a bottle of water off the shelf and gulps most of it down then perches on the table near the bed. "When I woke up and realized he had you too–" his voice cracks and he pauses, taking another gulp of water and clearing his throat. "There were so many emotions swirling in me, Ginger. I was angry, and afraid, and full of regret that our time might've been so short lived."

I sit up, this conversation clearly needing my full attention. Dane pushes up off the table and comes to kneel on the floor between my legs. He scoops my hands up into his own and kisses the back of each one. I pull one away and glide my fingertips through the hair that's trying to flop over his forehead.

"It's hard fer me to admit, but I've felt a little less incomplete since I met you, regardless of the mean front ya tried ta put on that first day. Yer pretty terrible at that, ya know that right?"

He smirks at me and it's beautiful, the way his eyes almost glitter despite their dark depths, the bit of crinkle in the corners and the upturn of just one side of his mouth.

"It's crazytown, but I feel like it was you I was waitin' on this whole time. Ya just hadn't found me yet."

Dane's head rocks into my stomach and he takes a deep breath in, and his arms wrap around my waist as mine cradle his head against me. He nuzzles into me and his hands dip into the back of the joggers he helped me into this morning. The tease of his fingers over my butt makes my body hum and I want more.

Dane must be feeling the same way because his hands turn the opposite way and push the sweater up my torso. His lips find my bare stomach and follow the hem upward until he's latched onto my nipple and is pulling the sweater over my head. He twists his tongue around the hardening peak as he sheds first his flannel, then his t-shirt, pulling off of me only long enough to get his head out then diving back in.

My hands run over his back, the taut muscles shuddering under my touch and his breathing changing the more passes my fingertips make across his neck. A low warning growl leaves Dane before he pulls my knees forward to wrap my legs around his waist and stands. I brace for him to drop me back onto the bed, but he doesn't, instead moving us to the wall. His hands run up my sides as he sets me in front of him and presses me into the wall with his hips, his erection pressing into my stomach as he invades my space and runs his nose up my throat and behind my ear.

My head drops back when his tongue runs over my pulse point and an involuntary whimper leaves me when he bites gently into my neck.

"Mmm," he hums. "The things I want to do to you every second I'm with you."

"Care to elaborate?" I prod.

Dane's head snaps up and his hand grabs my chin in a firm hold. His eyes bore into me and the fire in them could burn me from here. He presses his index finger into my mouth, pushing down on my tongue to force my mouth open. His nostrils flare and as much as my instinct is to close my mouth and either suck his finger to spur him on, or bite down to push back against his show of dominance, I allow him to force me into submission for the moment. Partly because I find this side of him delicious, and partly because I can feel his cock swelling harder behind his pants and I know my reward will be everything I want.

"I could start with you on your knees choking on my cock while tears spill down that beautiful face of yours.

Or…" his other hand shoves roughly into the back of my pants as he stoops down slightly, coming eye level to me and following my crack until he reaches my pussy. He runs a finger over me, spreading my lips to dip inside me before he sweeps the finger to my clit and runs a slow circle around it. "I could see how many times I can make you come before you're begging me to stop and Damien comes beating on the door."

He clasps my ass in his other hand, pulling me back off my feet and plunges the finger that was on my clit inside, rapidly pumping twice. I bite my lip to cut off my gasp. Dane's voice drops low when he presses his lips against my ear. "We're deep in the woods, Red, no one can hear you scream out here."

Unable to resist the wild urge, I turn my head and take his lips in a harsh, hurried kiss. The groan that builds low in his throat sounds like a growl and I deepen the kiss, pushing my way into his mouth. He drags deep breaths through his nose and pulls his hand out of my pants so he can work them off me. Dane's movements are frantic, and I relish in the knowledge that I make him this way.

When he has the pants off my cheeks he sets me back on my feet and I kick my way out of the pants. Dane presses me back into the wall and thrusts lazily against me, his hips rolling. I drop my gaze to watch his hips in their hypnotic dance. His hands cage me in on either side of my head, pressed into the wall and his head drops to my shoulder. I'm enjoying the cut muscle around his hip bones and the way his pants hang under them, the trail of hair that I know ends just over his girthy cock that's hiding barely below the pants that are tented and brushing my skin every time his fluid movements push him back into me in his slow, seductive dance. There's this feeling that builds low in my groin every time he slows things down and uses his body or his words to wind me higher before he breaks me apart and I swear it's a craving. It's a plea to indulge in more.

I reach between us, catching his cock in one hand and unbuttoning his pants with the other. I lock eyes with him when his head comes up and slowly glide the zipper down. I give him a gentle squeeze before grabbing both sides of his jeans by a belt loop and pull them down his hips. I follow the pants down, pooling them at his feet and gliding my fingers up the outsides of his thighs, stopping briefly to rub my tongue up the underside of his dick and give his head a little suck. He hisses and his hand catches in my hair with a tug. I freeze and look up at him. He's watching me with hooded eyes and flared nostrils, the very picture of the edge of control. I give his hip bone a little nip as I stand again, stopping to lick around one of his nipples before I bite gently over his collar bone and lick the seam of his lips.

Dane lunges forward at the contact with his lips, and holds me captive in a bruising kiss, using his hold on my hair to control my head. His other hand takes hold of my thigh and hooks it over his hip, my leg wrapping around him. He bends his knees and thrusts up in one swift move. I try to break away, but his grip tightens almost to the point of pulling my hair. He growls into my mouth as he continues to explore it with his tongue and nips his way to my lower lip.

Dane pulls my leg up higher around him, thrusting deeper as I struggle to stand on tiptoes. He thrusts harder, my back sliding up the wall and I cry out into his mouth at the bite of pain mixing with the intense thrumming happening inside me. He breaks the kiss and lets go of my head so he can bury his face in my neck and grab hold of my ass with his other hand, pulling me up off my foot and pressing my hips into the wall.

"Feel that, Red? Feel how perfectly my cock fills you? I was made for you, Ginger. And fuck if I can ever get my fill of you." He pounds rapidly into me before dropping me back to my feet, turning to walk me backward toward the bed.

He sits on the edge of the bed and urges me down to my knees before him. He doesn't have to tell me what he wants because I want it regardless. I close my lips over his head and he moans, his hands on my shoulders. I flatten my tongue and slide down his shaft, my own taste filling my mouth. When I hit the base of his cock I wiggle my tongue over him and he lets out a low curse. I bob on him, pushing him a little further back each time and soon enough Dane's hand is back in my hair. He holds me steady and his hips find their own pace, taking what he wants from me while I reach down to rub my aching clit, spurred on by the string of dirty words coming out of his mouth. There's nothing slow about the way I rub, nothing less than feral about the motions we're sharing and I climax quickly as he holds his cock in the back of my throat.

When Dane pulls my mouth off him, panting as hard as I am, he leans into me and devours my mouth, humming when my tongue meets his stroke for stroke. He helps me up off the floor, guiding me into his lap when he slowly pushes my hips over him, sinking into me as he brings my hand to his mouth and licks each of my fingers clean. The move is so erotic my stomach feels like it's fluttering while my walls clasp greedily around him.

When he's satisfied with my hands being free of my taste, Dane pushes back on my shoulders with one hand while the other supports my mid back. My head drops back as he leans in to chase my nipple, thrusting up into me while he rolls the bud around in his mouth. His strokes are slow and fluid, following the same dance he performed for me on the wall.

Little gasps leave me when he ends the rolls of his hips in short staccatos that leave me moaning after each intake of breath. He nips at the peak of my breast and snakes his free hand between us. Dane pinches my clit between his fingers and rolls it as his thrusts pick up speed and ferocity. The overwhelming sensations across my body send me careening over the edge of another climax, the sensation washing over my body from my pussy to my nipples and back again. His name leaves me in a hoarse scream and Dane chuckles as he rolls his head between my breasts.

"You're going to count for me, Red. How many is that, sweetheart?"

"One." I pant.

He quirks a brow at me.

"We shared that first one, doll. That was as much me as it was you, it don't count."

He laughs again and stands, flipping us around so my back is on the bed, but my head hangs slightly off. One of his knees comes up under my thigh and the other is planted on the ground.

"Game on," he whispers and plunges back inside. The pace he sets is intense and I can't match him, I can only be there to take it.

Dane catches a nipple in his fingers and pinches as he continues to pummel me. When I'm squealing more than I'm not, he puts the leg that's around him against his chest and leans into me further, changing the angle so he's thrusting over my g-spot and I shatter apart. My legs quake in a way I'm not used to and the urge to slam them together is so strong. Dane holds firm through my spasm and attempts to close him off, continuing until I'm climbing into another climax.

"Count, Ginger."

My back is arching off the bed, my legs bucking as the new orgasm builds. I moan, the sound long and guttural as I try to form words.

"Two!" I yell out and Dane grabs both of my legs, turning them to the side as he pulls his other leg up off the floor.

When he thrusts forward again he's positioned over me, sliding in and out on his knees, his pelvis bumping into my ass. The turn of his cock rubs the fat side of his head against my front wall and changes the sensation. He kneads my breast and slows down, dragging long, languid strokes over flesh that's quickly becoming far too sensitive. I wonder about the pace change as his arms shake and his moans become more frequent.

I try to turn again; to take control so I can make him as crazy as he's making me, but he holds my hip in place with a grunt. "I'm. Not. Finished. Here." Each word punctuated with another firm thrust until he's back to a pace that leaves him pistoning into me.

My breathing becomes erratic as I climb that peak higher and my head thrashes as my body begins to buzz.

"Never enough," Dane shakes out between groans and then he swats my ass. The sting makes me cry out but the burn morphs and wraps into the pleasure that's mounting and threatening to send me to my demise. His eyes seem to grow darker and he smacks my ass again, the burn sending me spiraling. My pussy clamps hard around him and I drag ragged breaths in as my eyes squeeze shut, every part of my body quivering and alive and beginning to sweat. The pleasure crashes through me with an overwhelming intensity and tears leak from the corners of my closed lids as I sob.

Dane rolls me to my back. "Three," he croons into my ear as his body envelops mine and he peppers kisses over my cheeks. He slides down my body, leaving searing hot kisses in his wake until his arms wrap around my thighs and his tongue glides up my slit.

"Oh my heaven above," I gasp out, my hips bucking up and spasming.

Dane moans and seals his mouth over me, his tongue lapping through me again and again while he sucks. I can't handle the intensity, the only sounds coming from me now are sobs as my body pulses, searching for something to take the edge off. My hands move to Dane's hair, pressing him tighter into me, searching for friction I already have that my body doesn't understand.

He sucks my clit between his teeth and my core tightens, a sensation I can feel up into my chest, robbing me of breath. "More," I plead. "Please, I need more, Dane. Please."

His lips leave me and I babble incoherently at him. "What's that, Red? I think I need you to ask me again." His fingers glide inside me and I think I might burst.

"Dane, please make me come. Please. Please." The word repeats as he continues to stroke.

"You're so fucking sexy when you beg."

His mouth clamps back over my clit, his tongue flicking over me rapidly before it traces down to meet his fingers. He scissors them, stretching my entrance and then his tongue wiggles inside, sweeping over me. This time I actually scream as my orgasm slams into me. Dane pulls his fingers out of me and shakes them vigorously over my clit and the orgasm intensifies until I'm shaking and suddenly do something I've never done before.

"Holy shit, Ginger. Fuck baby, did I just make you squirt?" A look of pure, satisfied amazement crosses his face and he climbs back onto the bed and thrusts himself into me. He's hard as a rock and thicker than I've ever felt him and the intense pleasure that immediately washes back over me is almost to the point of pain.

"Come fer me," I groan out.

He moans above me and his bottom lip sucks into his mouth. I can see him holding himself back, determined to drag this out even longer.

I lift my shoulders off the bed, my nails biting into his back as I pull myself up to his ear. "Dane, baby. I want you to come fer me. I wanna feel that rock hard cock pulse in my pussy and claim me as his. I wanna feel you fill me up while I touch the stars. Fuck me, Dane, please come in me."

Dane shudders and his rhythm falters when my head comes back down. He grunts and thrusts harder into me, his eyes watching me. "That was fucking hot."

I lick my lower lip then drag it into my mouth and grab a nipple with my fingers, twisting it and closing my eyes. He groans again and it's hard to keep my composure when I feel the rush of climax building again.

"Look at me," I command. His eyes open and I hold him there as I meet his next thrust. "Lemme feel that cock erupt. Show me whose pussy this is, Dane."

His control snaps and he fists the tit I'm not holding as he unleashes on me. His other hand holds my throat as his knees slide closer to change the angle and fit tighter against me. He squeezes my throat and I grit my teeth against the pleasure.

"That's right, baby, get that pussy." My next statement is cut short as I come again. I clamp and pulse around him and Dane lets out nothing less than a roar as he climaxes right behind me. He pumps a few more times then thrusts all the way in, holding himself there as his cock pulses inside of me and he desperately tries to draw a whole breath in.

He slowly releases my throat and runs his hands over my torso. "Dirty talk is *my* thing. But damn if I don't like it coming from your mouth."

"You didn't think ya were the only one with a filthy mouth, didya?"

He grins. It's sweet and carefree. A light chuckle breaks free, and he drops over me to place a kiss on my lips. "You stopped counting."

"Next time."

He nods and collapses onto the bed beside me. I turn into him, putting my head on his chest. He pulls me in tighter and drags his fingers lazily up and down my arm. This moment, this sensation, our skin together and his heartbeat sounding in my ear, it all feels so right.

CHAPTER TWENTY TWO

Dane

Ginger doses off as I stroke her arm, and I nearly do as well. My mind buzzes and a million things start racing through my thoughts, landing on the fact that Damien will probably be here in about twenty minutes, if I gauge how long we just spent tangled in each other correctly.

When she's softly breathing I carefully slip out from under her and put my clothes back on, heading outside to meet him before he wakes her. There's no road that will bring you all the way to the cabin set into the hills, so it's no surprise when I see his blonde head carefully working its way through the trees rather than headlights on a vehicle.

I stay at my post leaning against the door and Damien stops in front of me, fist held out for a bump that I oblige to.

"Glad to see you made it out and look intact. Sorry we didn't find you before the fire got too intense."

"It's alright," I assure him and kick off the wall. "I started it, I knew my way out."

"Holy shit, kid. *You* set the vault on fire? The fire took out half the compound. Fitzpatrick's men scattered, we were trying to nail down where they all went when you called."

'Scattered' is dangerous. They could be anywhere and ready for anything.

"What about Russell?" If he's out there, none of us are safe.

"Never saw him. Why?"

"I left him unconscious in the room he tied us up in."

"If he made it out, it was before we got there."

"Any idea how they knew where to find us?" It's been plaguing me since we got to the cabin. There's no way they should have known we were going to be there. Even if the men spotted us when we made it out to the street, how did they know which way we'd go back through? And why would they be ready to grab Ginger and Ellen when we hadn't reached the end of the demand time Russell had given us?

"Not sure yet," Damien shrugs. "But Jack is on it. He's running scans on everyone's phones from his position in Georgia and he's got James combing through data usage to look for spikes. Nothing yet. We still haven't ruled out a mole, we just have to figure out who."

"Who would've known we wanted Ginger with Ellen and Miriam other than me, you, James, Jack and Ginger?"

"Where did you talk to Ginger about it?" Damien asks after a moment of thought.

"In her room at the club. I wanted to go somewhere private where we couldn't be overheard. I figured it was safe. She said the room was only hers."

"We'll have to find out who has a key for that room if the phones all come up clean. Because if that's where the leak came from, that'll narrow things way down."

Damien shifts and looks around. "Where is Ginger anyway?"

"Inside, sleeping. Getting out of there was a nightmare, she's exhausted." Among other things.

"I'm surprised this place is still standing. We used to sneak out and party here. I don't know if anyone higher up even realizes this cabin exists. Or maybe they figure it's not an issue." Damien runs his hand on the wall of the cabin and looks lost in his memories.

"Give me two minutes and we'll be ready to get on the road. I want to get the hell away from here before nightfall. Especially if we don't know exactly where everyone dispersed to or if Russell and my dad made it out."

Damien salutes me and leans against the cabin. As I turn the knob on the door another thought occurs to me. "Has anyone checked on the apartments?"

"There's a team still in place there, and two at the lodge watching the women. They're our op teams from Towertech, guys we've had on staff since the beginning." He tilts his head, a silent question sounding at the end of his statement. But I don't have an answer for him, just a feeling. I make a sound of disinterest and step inside, closing the door behind me. Ginger is still in bed slumbering peacefully, naked, unbothered. Part of me wishes we could stay in this cabin, tucked away from the rest of the world, with a guarantee of safety. Because if I had it, I would never go back to the outside world. I'd just stay lost in her instead until the end of our days.

The resort is swarming in black clad bodies when we get back. The sun is low on the horizon and night is approaching as we pull up to a temporary block in the driveway.

"What're the odds we're bein' watched out here?" Ginger asks Damien as we're waved through the barricade and security radios ahead that we're coming.

"Pretty good, honestly. We did what we could to keep them off our tails, but we really have no way of knowing how far they followed us. Parameter sweeps come up clear, but we're on alert anyway."

"The club?" Ginger's face is stoic, but she's chewing her bottom lip, the only give away.

"Cleared out. Everyone is either here or already went south with Jack to check on his sister and their gran."

We make it up to the main lodge and the site is overwhelming. Barricades and vehicles block the route to the building, security lights high up on poles illuminate the space in front of them.

"How are the women taking this?"

Damien looks in the mirror, his eyes meeting mine and he sighs. "They seem mostly okay, a little spooked, but they're mostly grateful we're taking this seriously."

Ginger turns in her seat to face him. "What about those guys that was in the house when Russell's guys busted in and took me?" I hadn't considered that before now, there were two stationed there to keep Ellen safe.

Damien looks back to Ginger and shakes his head. "Eli didn't make it. Bear is in the hospital but he's going to be okay. They got the jump on them, shot through a window in the dining room. It's probably a good thing they didn't come through a door, Ellen might not have had the time she needed to get to the panic room. There's no telling what Russell would have done to her, even if she is carrying his grandchild."

"Where's she now?"

Damien parks the car in front of the main house and checks his watch. "If the chopper hasn't landed yet it should be just about to the helipad in Georgia. Jack had her brought down immediately. Honestly, she should've gone to begin with, but we didn't want them to act."

"Fat lot of good that did," Ginger mutters. I agree. Damien's grunt sounds like he's thirding the notion.

Ginger doesn't even get her door open all the way before Miriam comes pounding down the stairs to the porch and nearly tips Ginger over as she gets out of the car.

"I was so worried when they came back without you!" she sobs. When she pulls away she gasps and turns Ginger's head, exposing the burn on her throat. "Oh, honey. Oh. Let's go inside."

Damien steps up beside me as Miriam tucks Ginger into her side and they walk to the house. "Hey man, thanks for keeping her safe. Ginger means a lot to all of us."

"So I've learned. You know what though? She saved my ass. Swung a bat at a guy almost twice my size."

Damien's face breaks out into an amused grin. "No shit? Did she hit him?"

"No. He caught it. So she kicked him in the gut and then knocked his ass out when her knee connected with his chin." I really thought I was going to die in that hallway. My vision was tunneling, and my lungs were screaming, desperate for oxygen.

He nudges me with his elbow and takes a few steps forward. "Never let it be said she can't hold her own."

"I'm not interested in pissing her off any time soon, that's for sure."

Damien lets out a hearty laugh and jogs up the stairs. From outside the house looked dark, but inside it's like an operating room, with added bright lights everywhere, and people bustling around. There are several maps taped to walls with areas crossed off on them, presumably areas that have been swept and cleared.

"Where did all these people come from?" I ask, shocked at how full the room is after seeing all the men outside.

"There's a full security staff for the resort. A place this size? There has to be. Those are the guys watching the driveway in. The team at the lodge are James' guys, he's ex-ops and those were the guys he worked with. They were set up to cover the apartment when we got everyone moved in. He called them in early to watch everyone here. Everyone in here and out looking for Russell's guys are our security force for Towertech."

"That's the second time I've heard that. What's going on at Towertech that you need this kind of security?"

He shakes his head. "They're not for *protecting* Towertech, they work *at* Towertech. We hire out security, there's five teams. Jack called them all in."

Hired out security by one of the biggest tech companies on this side of the planet. It's no wonder his guys moved like SWAT through the compound when we went in to rescue everyone. It also makes sense why our dads are so hellbent on taking the company back if Jack's built up that kind of force and equipped them with the kind of advanced tech he has pumping out of there.

"Who's with Jack?"

Damien opens his mouth to answer when someone comes rushing in from the next room. "Got him!"

Everyone turns to look at the newcomer and he looks around the room, landing on Alex. "Russell, we found him and his brother, too. They're holed up at Jack's with a few other guys. Smart actually, we hadn't thought to look there until we got a security alert that the alarm had been down too long."

"That tracks." All eyes swivel to me. "They know Jack isn't there. It just makes sense they'd wait to ambush him. Has anyone checked Ginger's since everyone left?"

Alex considers me before speaking. "As of a few hours ago Ginger's was empty, and Phil says he hasn't seen anyone at the apartment complex. This is the only movement we've had, everything else we've checked is clear."

"What about nearby hotels?"

Alex cocks an eyebrow and his lips quirk up at the side. I'd like to think it's an impressed look. "We don't know all of the names, but we've run the names we do know and there's been no hits." He turns back to the man who brought us the news. "Send a unit to extract, if possible. I don't want any of ours fallen, got it? If they can't do it safely, they don't go in."

"And the other side?" he asks.

"Take them out." Alex was poised to speak but I beat him to it. He stares at me, jaw still open. "They'll never stop. If they can't be taken, put them down. It's the only way to keep people safe. In fact, I'll go along."

"You aren't trained," Alex interjects.

"On the contrary. I know exactly what they'll do, because they taught me to do it."

"No." His face is stern.

"I'm going," I tell him before I walk away.

"Ya really thinkin' that's a good idea?" I pause when I hear her voice. Ginger is standing behind me on the other side of the wall attached to the doorway that separates the kitchen from the sitting room.

Head in my hands I turn around and scrub them down my face. "I can't let them keep terrorizing people. It's eating me on the inside and if someone else gets taken or killed. I can't–"

I feel like I can't breathe. I drag an unsteady breath through my nose and Ginger steps into my body, wrapping me in her delicate arms, her head on my chest. The feel of her wrapped around me steadies me and I hold her back.

"I can't live with that." The end comes out in a whisper and she holds me tighter.

"You do whatcha gotta do then. Ya do it and then ya come back, you understand me?" Her gaze finds mine and I see something there I haven't seen before. A real concern that comes from somewhere deeper. No one has ever looked at me like that and it squeezes my chest.

"Yes, ma'am," I tell her with a grin.

She scoffs and gives my chest a shove but I pull her closer as I rock forward again, snatching her hands in mine and kissing her softly.

"I promise."

CHAPTER TWENTY THREE

Ginger

It's been three hours. Three hours since Dane promised he would be back. Three hours since I watched the black van drive away full of men.

These kinds of missions aren't what I'd call a normal occurrence, but they also aren't unheard of. I know they know what they're doing but that doesn't mean I'm not pacing the room listening to the seconds on the clock tick.

Exhaustion is starting to set in and I'm just dozing off in the chair I plopped in when I hear the door to the study open. My eyes snap open and Dane is standing there. His hair is disheveled and his uniform is ripped open. There's a gash over his collar bone but he looks otherwise okay aside from the wild look on his face.

He takes a shaky step forward and it's like I wake up all at once. I bolt out of the chair and into his arms where he all but collapses into me. I take his weight for a few seconds, then slowly sink us to the floor as sobs start racking his body. I let him cry, let the gates on the anguish he's been feeling flow so his tears can wash him clean.

"Wanna talk about it?" I ask when he's taking deeper breaths and his body relaxes.

"They're gone. They took a shot at Jay and the team opened fire. They're both gone."

"Oh, honey. I'm sorry."

He shakes his head, sniffling and sitting up straight with a sigh. "I'm not. I mean, part of me feels it out of a sense of obligation. But they weren't good men, they've killed a lot of other people. But I'm not."

"What does it mean then? The two of thems bein' gone."

"Hard to say. It depends on the generals. It's unlikely they'll reconvene here; they'll likely move west to another bigger compound. It should be over here. For a while, anyway."

I nod my head, not wanting to jinx the thought. "It's okay ta be sad ya know. Even when the memories are bad ones. I still miss my mom despite all the shit she put me through and bein' absent all the time and mean when she was around. Doesn't make it hurt no less. That's okay."

Dane nods and clears his throat. "It's fine," he says and stands then holds his hand out to me. "I'd rather move forward."

EPILOGUE

Dane

"That's the last of it." I wipe my hands off on my jeans and look around the room. We spent the last week working with Phil's teams to get the apartments finished. It was a lot of work, a lot more than anyone anticipated, especially after the new electrical when we had to start putting new walls in where the wires had previously been ripped right through them. We tried to track down the mole, flush out whoever sold us out to the Fitzpatrick compound to no avail. So, we moved forward with the plans for safety we all agreed to and put a few extra cameras on the exterior perimeter of the building to try to catch danger before it comes inside. It became overwhelming, moving between the ski resort and the apartments on a constant basis, and everyone was burnt out by the end of it.

But the soft grey walls and the pretty blue couches in this room with the plants scattered around and the new bookshelves with a few classics to start a collection out are quite the sight for sore eyes. It speaks to the dedication everyone gave. It's a huge reminder of where everyone came from, and how far they can go.

"Not quite." Ginger crosses the room and pushes a stake into the plant on the low table under the window.

I move closer and take a look. "Grow through what you go through." I read the little bulb at the top of the stake and Ginger tucks under my arm. "It's perfect," I tell her and kiss the top of her head.

"Should we go get 'em?"

"Yeah, I think we should."

The women and the little kids are all outside in the green space behind the building. Picnic tables were brought in to give them space to congregate when it's nice outside and to let the kids play on the equipment we collected from resale places.

"Who wants to go inside?" Ginger calls out with a smile. The kids all decline with a collective groan and several laughs follow them.

Damien and Miriam meet Ginger at the door with the list and the keys to distribute as everyone walks inside. Jack and Ellen, Alex and Christie, James and all the other guys are already inside to help with any issues. When the last of the women tearfully thank Miriam for her new keys we all step through the threshold ourselves, making up the caboose.

Ginger and I stop in each apartment, sometimes just to chat and listen to its occupants and their excited thanks, sometimes to help move furniture or jot down what else they need. Ginger is in her element here, hustling and bustling and simply helping.

I watch her rearrange a pair of armchairs after she swatted away my help and I know how I fell for her even when I insisted I was immune. It's her determination. It's the depth of love in her eyes despite all the things she's been through in her life and the fight she's willing to put up for the people around her. And those people around her are absolutely endless.

"I think I love you, Red," I confess when she tucks herself back into my side.

Her head snaps up so her wide eyes can lock with mine. "What'd ya just say?"

"I think you heard me."

"I think I must've passed out movin' those chairs and now I'm dreamin' on tha floor."

I shake my head with a chuckle. "It's not a big thing. It's just a feeling. I think I love you."

"How do you decide if you can be sure or not?" A grin spreads across her face.

I pull my wrist up, checking a watch that's not there but knowing we're only a few hours from sunset. "Looks like we've got plenty of time to figure it out."

"Oh, that was bad." She laughs.

"I'm just getting started," I tell her, and pull her in for a kiss.

www.ingramcontent.com/pod-product-compliance
Lightning Source LLC
Chambersburg PA
CBHW051956150726
47999CB00004B/1413